Southern Thyme Catering Co.

With Salsa on the Side

Thyme is on our side!
Marsha Thauwald

Written by Marsha Thauwald
Illustrated by Laryssa Barbalat

ISBN: 978-1-5356-1632-4

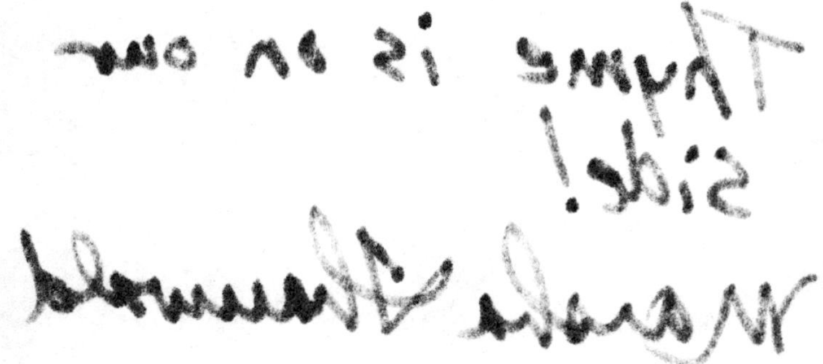

Dedication

This book is dedicated to all public servants—teachers, preachers, doctors, nurses, paramedics, and military personnel. Without their dedication to their chosen careers, we would be in a world of hurt. Thank you for all that you do every day!

Endorsements

This third book of Marsha's has a twist that keeps you engaged until the very end! Once I started reading, I couldn't put the book down! What a wonderful end to the trilogy about the family and friends of Cora Jean and Cara Louise!

– Becca Bell,
"Bebe" to Braxton, Cannon, and Saydi, AND a great friend to so many others!

I thoroughly enjoyed reading this new book! How fun it was to connect the past, present, and future stories of the Trinity women in the latest read, *Southern Thyme Catering Company*. The "future" characters are just as colorful and engaging as the past, with a storyline that drew me in and kept me reading! Everyone needs a little "salsa on the side" to spice things up and keep life interesting. This latest book in the *Southern Thyme Mystery Series* does just that!

– Sue Connor,
Friend and Southern Resident by Choice!

Southern Thyme Catering Company is an outstanding story about a determined young woman who opens her own restaurant and catering company in a small town in Arizona. The story involves her love for family, faith, the past, new friends, an intriguing mystery, suspense, and a little romance, all woven together around the central theme of "thyme!" It is an enjoyable read and I highly recommend it!

– Georgia Power,
Teacher, Counselor, Administrator, Drill Team Sponsor, and Lifelong Friend

Acknowledgements

For some reason, this segment of the book is always my favorite. It's not one that most people read; however, putting our gratitude on paper makes the thankfulness even more heartfelt.

First of all, I want to thank my family and friends who have taken the "thyme" to make the story better: Pete Thauwald, Becca Bell, Sue Connor, Marianne Lanman, and Georgia Power.

Secondly, thanks to the salsa-recipe creators: Deborah Hernandez, Pete Thauwald, Micah Kroll, Kim Hefner, Robin O'Neil, Monica Lopez, Theresa Hale, Dick and Marcia Salgado, Vonda Warren, Elizabeth Hostin, and the *Fort Worth Star-Telegram* Home & Garden section.

Much appreciation goes to my friends who allowed me to use their names as characters in the book: Becca, Saydi, Maia, Zoë, Pete, Brother Dan, Lois, Jarrett, Mary Tom, and Tallulah.

Thanks to Sarah and Shirley, owners of A New Chapter—Books on the Square, located in Mansfield, Missouri, for giving me permission to use the title of their bookstore in the epilogue.

Finally, thanks be to God, who has been my ultimate inspiration for writing.

Contents

Southern Thyme Catering Co.

With Salsa on the Side

Prologue

December 31, 2042

As I sit here and think about all that has happened in the last two years I can't help but remember what's important in life: faith, family, and freedom—and maybe my favorite foods. Looking through old photo albums as tears roll down my cheeks, I realize just how lucky my family and I have been. Re-reading old letters and gazing at pictures that will forever be deeply rooted in my heart, I know that God has raised me to be a strong-willed woman just like my mom, my grandmother, Aunt Cara, and the Trinity women before them. They were always moving forward…

June 29, 1980

Dear Cara,I can hardly wait for August to get here because that's when you will be here in person!

Guess what? Aunt Lottie and I bought Della's Diner. And guess what else? We changed the name to Jean and

Joe's Place. I got the idea when I came to help with the Whistle Stop Café's 50th anniversary two years ago. It's a way to bring a little bit of Daddy to Truway. Don't you know that Mama and Daddy would be so proud to have a place of their own?

You will also be glad to know that I ran into Austin Chilacothe last week and we had a good talk. He plans to take over his grandfather's farm in the fall. He asked if I would have lunch with him sometime, so I told him I would. That was three lunches ago. We sit in the back booth in the café and talk about his plans for Chilacothe farm and my plans for Big Southern Hair & Highlights beauty salon.

Not only will we make our traditional trips to the cemetery and see Mrs. Chilacothe, we will be celebrating the 50th anniversary of the salon! I had a plaque made to put on one of the hairdryers which reads "Big Southern Hair & Highlights--1930–1980."

It's time to turn in so I will close for now. It will be wonderful to see you again. Give Aunt Thelma and Sam a BIG hug from me. You are such a blessing in my life!

Love you forever,

CJ

July 10, 1980

Dear CJ,

It was so good to hear from you! I am excited that our annual get-together is just around the corner. I'll be in Truway in exactly a month and look forward to the Big Southern Hair's 50th anniversary.

It was great to read that you and Aunt Lottie bought Della's Diner and changed the name to "Jean and Joe's Place"! It sounds like you're doing a lot for the economy in town. I'm thrilled that you ran into Austin and you two are spending worthwhile time together. He has always been a good friend and no matter what happened in the past or what will happen in the future, he will be someone who has your back.

I have lots of things to share with you. First of all, Glen sends his love. His cardiologist says that his heart is better than he first thought. Glen would benefit from a heart transplant in the future, but he may not be an eligible candidate to get on a list. We have decided to spend a few years on the ranch until he gets stronger. Aunt Thelma is so happy that we're here. You will never guess what we found out. There's going to be a Marfan's Syndrome Foundation in Port Washington, New York! Can you believe it! It will be finished early next year, and the founding members have asked Glen and me to attend the ribbon-cutting ceremony!

We are extremely proud to attend. Since we came up with the idea to have a Marfan's Syndrome Camp at Las Bonitas Ranch each summer, it is only natural to advertise its existence through the Foundation. We plan to host the first camp next June.

Not only do we want the people with Marfan's to visit a week at a time, we want to invite their family members, too.

I already painted the sign that I want hung at the front gate. It is only right to put Sam on the sign. After all, he has saved my life more than once and I want to honor him. He will be a big attraction to the future campers.

I don't have any other news at this time. It will be great to see you next month. Until then, give my love to Aunt Lottie, take care, and know that I thank God for you every day!!

Love that never fails,
CARA

CJ is my grandmother and Cara is my great-aunt. They have experienced so much in their lives. They were twins born just a few minutes apart, but separated for most of their formative years. When they finally met at fourteen they got to share their mom's diary and found out how she died mysteriously. In their adult lives they discovered that their grandmother, Betsy Grace, a famous singer, also lost her life prematurely.

Through it all, the twins stayed close while living hundreds of miles apart in two different states, New Mexico and Texas. Their letters to each other show their devotion throughout their lives:

September 4, 2016

Dear Cara,

It was so great to see you this summer. I'm excited about seeing you again at Christmas. Ashley and Sam plan to be married on Christmas Eve, but said they wouldn't go on their honeymoon until after Christmas Day so we can spend it together.

Life is busy, but good. Chilacothe Farms is thriving and everyone is doing well. We are blessed!

Aunt Lottie sends her love. I look forward to hearing what's going on in New Mexico. Eat a Jean's Delight taco at the Whistle Stop Café for me. Thank you for being the best twin sister a girl could have!

Love that never fails,

CJ

Jean was my greatgrandmother and the namesake of Jean's Delight, a specialty at the Whistle Stop Café. I never got to meet her, since she died right after the twins were born. I've been told that I look like her, slim with high cheekbones, sky-blue eyes, and a mess of curly darkbrown hair. Most of the time I wear it pulled up and out of the way. As I continue to reminisce, it's fun to read how email was a great way to communicate back in 2016, but even today, handwritten letters are the best.

September 11, 2016

Dearest CJ,

I treasure your letters. It's so wonderful to go to the mailbox and see your handwriting on an envelope. We're counting the days until Christmas when we'll all be together again witnessing the beautiful union between Ashley and Sam. Guess what? Glen surprised me with a very unique gift yesterday. I guess I should reference them as two gifts. One appeared behind him and the other on his left side. Their names are Tuck and Jess and they are miniature burros from the Sicilian line of donkeys. I call them my little burritos. Tuck is a buff color and Jess's coat is a reddish brown. Both of our new friends have a darkbrown cross on their backs which makes them even more special. They won't be able to take Sam the snow-white burro's place in my heart, but I'm sure they will carve out their own space. I can hardly wait for all of you to visit next summer so I can show them to you. I have enclosed pictures for you to see. I ate a Jean's Delight for you and it was delicious. Kiss Aunt Lottie for me.

Love you forever,

Cara

P.S. Tell Ashley that I never told her how happy I am that she met another Sam. It was meant to be!

Ashley is my mom and Sam, my dad. They help my grandmother, CJ, whom I lovingly refer to as Grandma Cora, take care of the family businesses in Texas. Aunt Cara lived on the ranch and helped with the summer activities for Victory Bound Campground until her death ten years ago.

I live just outside Willcox, Arizona, in the small town of Reverence, near the western New Mexico border. My name is Trinity Grace Taylor, owner of the Southern Thyme Catering Company. I've always wanted to own my own restaurant. People seem to connect with others over a mouthwatering meal. My specialty is thyme dishes that I've been creating for many years thanks to mentor chefs who have allowed me to use their recipes. As a matter of fact, the best of these recipes is found in salsas that I've shared with family and friends, most of whom are also my customers.

Right at this moment I'm feeling blessed to still be alive. The past two years have been, as Charles Dickens would say, "the best of times and the worst of times..."

Jean & Joe's PLACE

Chapter 1: Southern Thyme Catering Company, "OPENING SOON!"

Deborah's Thyme for Peaches

2 firm but ripe peaches
2 fresh jalapeños
½ small Vidalia onion
5 sprigs fresh lemon thyme
5 dried apricots, chopped
¼ cup club soda
½ lemon

Soak the apricots overnight in club soda. The next day pull leaves off the thyme. Chop the remainder of the ingredients, except lemon. Add to the bowl of apricots. Add juice from the lemon. Mix ingredients until a slight sauce is created. Serve with your favorite chips.

I couldn't believe I was standing in front of my very own establishment. It was amazing that I was now the proprietor of Southern Thyme Catering Company, *with salsa on the side!* Opening day would be Valentine's Day, February 14, 2040. Owning restaurants ran in my family. My great-grandfather was the chef of the Whistle Stop Café in Whistle Stop, New Mexico. Della's Diner in Truway, Texas, was purchased by my great-great-great-aunt Lottie and renamed Jean & Joe's Place in memory of my great-grandparents. My mom and Grandma Cora still ran Jean & Joe's Place.

The restaurant and catering company would be open for business six days a week, only closing on Sundays. Today I would begin the search for a chef and three waitstaff people. I checked the weekly *Reverence Rally* online newspaper to reread the ad letting the locals know a new place was opening in our quaint little town.

> *Southern Thyme Catering Company "OPENING SOON!" in Reverence. Trinity Grace Taylor is seeking outgoing, friendly people to help her operate her new restaurant. Prospective team members must be willing to smile for up to eight hours at a time and only applicants with a strong work ethic need*

apply. Please call 555-777-5000 to schedule an interview.

As I sat in a rocker on the front porch of the restaurant reading the ad out loud, a shadow appeared, blocking the view on my screen. I looked up and saw a petite young woman smiling at me.

"Are you here to interview for a position?" I asked.

"Yes, I'm hoping you want to hire me to be your personal assistant even though you didn't advertise for one. I can wait tables if I need to; however, I just got my associate's degree in business and plan to continue with a four-year degree in business management in the future. I need to work so I will have money to continue my education. I think you're going to need someone to take care of your books, events, and payroll for the other workers," she said in a confident voice.

"Why don't you tell me your name and then we can talk about your qualifications." I smiled.

"My name is Jo Ellen Butler. I live in Willcox now but was raised on the Rancho del Sol just west of here, so I know everyone in the county and believe I would be a good marketing asset for you."

"I like your confidence, Jo Ellen. Let's go inside and talk more about your goals and I'll see if they are in line with mine. Would you like a cup of coffee? It's

Southern pecan––one of the coffee choices we will serve every day," I said as I got up and walked inside.

I liked Jo Ellen right away. We were so preoccupied in our conversation that we didn't hear the bell ring above the door as someone walked in, startling us both.

"May I order breakfast?" the stranger asked.

"Oh, I didn't hear you come in. Actually, we're not open yet," I replied.

"Well, your door was open so I say it's okay to walk in, don't you?" he asked with his eyebrows raised.

"I can't fix you breakfast until we officially open on February fourteenth, but I can get you a complimentary cup of coffee." I smiled.

"Coffee is good, but I sure would like to eat something, too," he sighed as he looked around the room.

"Ms. Taylor, will you allow me to go to Mel's Market and get some bacon and eggs for Otis?" Jo Ellen asked.

"Otis, huh? Have you lived in Reverence long?" I asked instead of answering Jo Ellen.

"I've lived here all my life with Silas," he responded proudly.

"Who's Silas?" I continued.

"He's my brother and he looks just like me." Otis grinned.

"Are you twins?"

Before he could answer me, the bell chimed again as someone who indeed looked just like Otis walked through the door.

"Excuse me. I thought I saw my brother walk in here. I realize you're not open for business yet, but he was so curious about seeing this place and I couldn't make him understand that we couldn't eat here yet," Otis's brother said as his face blushed three shades of red.

"You must be Silas. Otis was just telling me about you," I said as I extended my hand to shake his.

As he took my hand, Jo Ellen spoke up and said, "Silas, this is Trinity Taylor, the owner of Southern Thyme Catering Company."

"It's so nice to meet you, Trinity, but I have a question. Why do you call your place 'Southern Thyme Catering Company' when you live in the Southwest?" Silas asked.

"I was raised most of my life in Texas, which I consider part of the South, so it made sense to me that the name of my first restaurant would describe my heritage. It's surprising that you're not asking why 'Thyme' is spelled the way it is," I explained.

"That was going to be my next question," Silas said as his shades of red got even darker.

"My grandfather's family grew thyme on their farm in Truway just outside of Del Rio for generations. It only seemed right for me to pay tribute to Chilacothe Farms by having 'Thyme' in the title.

I also plan to serve many dishes that have thyme in them, especially unique salsa recipes," I said.

"Thanks for the explanation. May I send my friend George over to interview you about how your restaurant got its name? I think the folks in Reverence would like to read about your history, and it'll be good for business," Silas said.

"Of course. Jo Ellen, will you go over to Mel's Market and get us some breakfast items to fix for our guests?"

"See, Silas. I told you I could eat breakfast here today," Otis said as he grinned from ear to ear.

* * *

Later, I found myself back in the rocking chair on the front porch of my restaurant, which unofficially opened today for a brief time to celebrate new friends. Jo Ellen would be my personal assistant, as she'd hoped. I knew she'd be instrumental in getting everyone interested in eating here on a regular basis. She said she planned to create marketing flyers for us to use right away. Otis and Silas said they would spread the word about the grand opening. George from the *Reverence Rally* newspaper would be here tomorrow to talk to me about how the restaurant got its name and find out more about me.

All in all, today was a huge success. I not only hired Jo Ellen, but I also found a chef. Gabe moved out here from New York, where he worked with top chefs in the city. He said he needed to leave the Big Apple so he could see more of America. He stopped by Gus's Station to plug in his electric car and was told that a new restaurant was opening up in town. He showed up right after Jo Ellen left this morning.

Two other new team members came in for interviews.Maia would be a hostess and would help the new waitress, Mary Tom, serve the guests. We'd postpone hiring someone else until we had enough customers. I couldn't believe my great fortune in finding these quality people to help me in putting Southern Thyme Catering Company on the map.

* * *

Feeling restless after a rewarding day, I decided to take a stroll down Main Street and peer through the store windows. They were all closed for the day, but it didn't hurt to get a sense of the owners' tastes by looking in the windows of their shops.

I walked by Mel's Market, run by none other than Mel himself. He had called and said that he wanted to talk to me about ordering supplies through him. He had been in business here the longest. Next to Mel's was Slim Pickens Mercantile. The owner was named after the famous cowboy and movie actor. The sign on his door said, “Come on in, sit a spell, and talk to me about the good ole days.”

Across from the market was Twinkle City Laundromat, operated by Lois Tull, a part-time flag dancer for the church at the end of the street. I liked the name Lois picked out for the laundromat. Looking through her big picture window, I saw two rows of washers and dryers. I’d be using her big machines to launder the linen napkins and tablecloths from the restaurant. Everything was programmed digitially.

Across from Twinkle City was the county courthouse in the center of the square, and on the other side of the street was the Reverence Pioneer Days Library and Museum, started by Becca Ellis, who was still the curator. Jo Ellen said that Becca once worked at the renowned Rex Allen Museum in Willcox before it became the City Hall. The Rex Allen showcased Arizona’s only remaining original Southern Pacific Railroad depot, which was constructed in 1881. The library and museum in Reverence were also known for the early settlers’ history.

I’d visited the museum on my first visit to town but was unable to meet Becca at the time. The displays inside were amazing, especially the window display. There was a platform that had an old school desk and slate on one end. On the other end was a sack of grain sitting in the bed of a small wagon. Above the wagon was a board with old cooking supplies nailed on it. Just as I was turning to leave and walk back to my porch, I saw what I thought was a man standing behind the display. As I cupped my hands around my eyes and stuck my nose to the glass to get a better view, I realized it couldn't be a person because he wasn't moving. Then I remembered that the museum had several mannequins sitting and standing around to make the scenes more realistic. Becca must have put this mannequin up front for some reason, but it didn't seem to belong with everything else. I'd have to come back tomorrow tomeet Becca and ask her about the mannequin.

There was one place not within walking distance that I would get to visit tomorrow, too, the Oasis Club & Resort, owned by Silas Warner. Silas had been the town sheriff for many years and decided to retire and open the resort. He and Otis had invited me to lunch. I was anxious to check out my competition. Silas said that he thought Reverence was big enough to handle both eating establishments. As a matter of fact, he said that he would like for us to join forces when it came to catering special events. I certainly hoped so, because I was raring to make a go of Southern Thyme Catering Company. That was why "Catering Company" was part of the title too, since I wanted to accommodate unique affairs in town and maybe even in Willcox.

I decided to go up to my apartment above the restaurant and try out one of the salsa recipes I planned to share with customers and then call it a night. Tomorrow was going to be one of many busy days. I looked forward to lunch at the Oasis with Otis and Silas and the possibility of meeting Becca at the museum. My plan was to take them a potted lemon thyme plant as a token of my appreciation for being embraced as a new member of the Reverence community.

Later, as I closed my eyes and waited to drift off into a restful sleep, the last thing on my mind was how the mannequin in the museum window seemed familiar.

Southern Thyme Catering Co.

Chapter 2: An Oasis and a Museum in the Desert

Pete's Hot Sauce

1 can whole peeled tomatoes

1 can tomato sauce

1 can tomato paste

2 small Roma tomatoes, sliced

½ small yellow onion

1–2 jalapeños

2 dashes Tabasco sauce

3 shakes salt and pepper

1 clove garlic

3 sprigs garden thyme

1- 2 tablespoons chopped cilantro (to taste)

Blend all ingredients in blender for 30 seconds on medium-high speed.

Jo Ellen was already sitting at one of the tables when I walked down the stairs the next morning. "You're here at the crack of dawn. Why so early?" I asked as I headed to the kitchen.

"I couldn't sleep. Ideas for promotional posters kept popping up in my head. I tried counting sheep so that I could shut down my brain, but every time I envisioned a lamb jumping over a fence, I saw pictures of food features instead," Jo Ellen replied.

"Food features?" I asked.

"What do you think about having a 'food feature' every day? Most restaurants call them 'daily specials,' but I wanted us to be different," she continued.

"I'm willing to see what you have in mind on paper. Since you're here, why not develop a few posters for us to discuss when I get back this afternoon?" I said.

"I will. We only have two weeks before opening day so I want to get started right away. How about a side salsa feature, too, or do you want to have several salsas available for people to try every day?" Jo Ellen's creative ideas just kept coming.

"Let's do both. Let's have one featured salsa every day, but also allow our customers to try different ones before ordering what they like," I answered.

"Great idea. Thanks so much for giving me the opportunity to work with you. Southern Thyme Catering Company is going to be the most famous restaurant in the state of Arizona." She smiled.

"Speaking of restaurants what can you tell me about the Oasis Club & Resort? I asked. I'm going to have lunch with Silas and Otis today."

"Silas built it from the ground up after retiring from being the Reverence sheriff. He never married and had no family of his own since he's taken care of Otis most of his life, so he must have saved a lot of money over the years. He came up with the idea of starting the club and then added on the resort a short time later. The people in town were surprised to see how well off he seemed to be since the salary of a town sheriff isn't much, but everyone was happy for him and Otis.

"Most of his business comes from out of town. Different organizations book the resort for their annual retreats. Families also reserve their reunions there. The club is open every evening and showcases bands from all over the country on weekends," Jo Ellen responded.

"Tell me more about Otis. Why does Silas need to take care of him?" I asked.

"Otis was born a couple of minutes after Silas. The story is that the doctor didn't know their mom was having twins. She went into labor after only six months of pregnancy. Her husband called the doctor to come to their house rather than driving her to the Mountain View Mercy Hospital.

"The doctor was a neighbor and was only too glad to take a short drive to their home to check on her. By the time he arrived, it was too late to get her to the hospital. The doctor delivered Silas almost immediately and thought everything was going fine until Mrs. Warner insisted there was another baby. He argued with her and said it was her imagination. Mr. Warner asked him to look again and sure enough, Otis's head was crowning, but he wasn't able to make it through the birth canal without help. The umbilical cord was wrapped around his neck and his oxygen was cut off. The doctor revived him, but as a result, Otis is what some people call 'slow.' He went to school with Silas, but never learned to read or write well. The Warners later put him in a special-education setting at the school, where he mastered life skills. When Silas graduated from high school he started working for the City of Reverence and got Otis a job with the maintenance crew.

"Their parents died in a car accident soon after, so Silas and Otis have been side by side every day at home and work," Jo Ellen explained.

"Thanks. I'm lucky to have you around to keep me informed so that I don't offend anyone with my questions." I smiled and finally sauntered into the kitchen to get a cup of coffee. I would have to come up with a name for a special coffee that featured either Reverence or Arizona in the title, like the famous tea company in the state.

* * *

I didn't tell Jo Ellen about the mannequin I'd seen in the window last night. Maybe my mind was playing tricks on me, because now that I was sitting in my car by the curb and peering inside, the mannequin wasn't there.Taking a deep breath, I got out of the car, rehearsing in my head how I would bring up the mannequin to Becca. The picture-window display was the same minus the "man" standing behind it.

I must have been staring intently at the display, because I didn't hear someone walk up to me until she asked, "May I help you find something?"

Jumping at the sound of her voice, I laughed nervously. "I'm sorry. I was so deep in my thoughts I didn't hear you come up to me. I'm not usually this skittish. Please forgive me," I replied.

"That's quite all right. My name is Becca Ellis. I'm the museum curator." She smiled.

She was around five feet five inches tall with big blue eyes and thick dark hair. Her smile was contagious. I smiled back at her and said, "My name is Trinity Taylor. I'm the owner of the soon-to-be open Southern Thyme Catering Company down the street."

"I've heard about your restaurant. We're all excited about your grand opening in a couple of weeks. I'm glad you came in. I thought it would be fun to put a few of the pieces from our museum displays in the restaurant so that people from out of town would know to visit us after they eat at your restaurant. What do you think about that idea?" she asked.

"It's ingenious. Speaking of displays, I have a question about your picture window. Last night I was walking around town and looked through your window. I thought I saw a man standing behind your display. As I peered closer, I could tell he wasn't a real man, maybe a mannequin. But I don't see it here this morning," I said, trying to hide the embarrassment in my voice.

"Hmm, I didn't put a mannequin by the front window. Let me ask Saydi. She was here yesterday. I just got back in town from a conference in Tucson. Saydi, did you put a mannequin by the front window for some reason yesterday?" Becca asked.

"No, I didn't. There has never been a mannequin by the front window. Maybe you're referring to the cowboy I put by the covered wagon at the back," Saydi replied.

They both turned and looked at me for what seemed like ages before I spoke up. "Obviously, I'm mistaken. Yesterday was a long day and I must've been seeing things, but just to satisfy my curiosity, may I see the cowboy by the covered wagon you mentioned?"

Saydi led the way as we walked to the back of the museum. The cowboy didn't look anything like the mannequin I'd seen last night. I decided I'd describe him. "The one I saw last night didn't have on a hat. He was wearing jeans with a bright red shirt and vest. He seemed to have receding gray hair and a beard. I couldn't see his feet."

"That sounds a lot like our head maintenance man, Walt, but he wouldn't have been here past six. As a matter of fact, he hasn't shown up for work this morning. I was going to ask you if he called in sick." Saydi turned and looked at Becca.

"No, I didn't hear from Walt. Once he comes in we'll ask him if he worked late last night. What makes you think the man standing behind the window display wasn't real?" Becca asked.

"He appeared to be stiff like a statue. He wasn't moving at all. If he'd been a real person, I think he would have made eye contact with me or at least waved or something," I said with exasperation.

"We'll clear up your mystery, Trinity. Would you like for me to show you around the museum? We have other displays showcased that include mannequins dressed for events we want to portray," Becca said.

"Maybe some other time? I'm on my way to have lunch at the Oasis Club & Resort. I do want to talk more about putting some of the museum items in the restaurant. How about dinner next week to discuss what you have in mind?" I asked hurriedly.

"Sure. I'll talk to Walt about yesterday and either call you or drop by to look at your restaurant in the next few days so we can come up with some ideas when we have dinner," Becca said.

As I got to my car, I turned and looked back at the museum. Becca and Saydi were standing in the door staring at me. I was sure they were wondering what I thought I saw last night. If I was lucky, they wouldn't judge me after meeting me, but first impressions were important. Maybe I did see Walt and maybe he didn't see me peering through the window, or just maybe I'd been working way too hard lately.

* * *

The Oasis Club was further out of town than I'd expected, but I still arrived about ten minutes prior to my luncheon engagement. Otis was standing on the front steps waving at me before I even stopped the car. When I was about to get out, he appeared and opened the door for me., "Welcome to our place!" he said excitedly.

"Hello, Otis. I'm glad to be here. Where's Silas? Didn't he want to be a part of the greeting committee?" I laughed.

"There's not a committee, just me." He smiled broadly.

I chuckled at his comment and then stopped. I didn't want him to think I was making fun of him. He started laughing too, and then ushered me up the steps and into the club. "Silas, Trinity is here!" he exclaimed.

Silas came from a different room, wiping his hands on a dishtowel. "Yes, I see," he said.

"Hi, Silas. I know I'm a little early, but that's the way I roll. My grandmother always said, 'if you're not at least five minutes early, you're late.'" I laughed again.

"It's a good thing, too, because Otis has been standing on those steps watching for you to arrive since the sun came up this morning," Silas said.

"The sun wasn't up when I went outside. I got to watch it come up while I was sitting in the rocking chair on the front porch. We have a rocking chair just like you, Trinity," Otis said as he walked back out, expecting me to follow him.

I went outside and sat in his chair and said, "This chair is almost identical to mine. Where did you get yours?"

"It belonged to our mother. It's Otis's favorite place to sit," Silas said.

"My chair belonged to my great aunt, Cara, and before that it belonged to her great aunt, Thelma. She lived on a ranch in New Mexico and oversaw the Victory Bound Campground. I think Otis would love the campground," I said.

"Can I go to the Victory Bound Campground someday, Silas?" Otis asked.

"Maybe someday, but right now I need to attend to our lunch preparation so I can impress Trinity," Silas responded.

Lunch was indeed impressive. We had crab cakes with a special kind of sauce, grilled asparagus, and a salad made with cranberries, walnuts, blue-cheese sprinkles, and homemade dressing. Otis let me know that he'd made the tea and lemonade. He mixed them together and called it Otis's Sunshine Drink. Everything was delicious.

"So, Silas, what do you serve when you have groups staying at the resort?" I asked.

"I send a list of menu items to the group contact several weeks before they arrive and let them check off what they would like to have while staying here," he replied.

"I love what you served today. Is this meal on your list?" I asked.

"No, I made this particular meal just for you. The things I serve are foods like enchiladas, fajitas, chicken-fried steak, or hamburgers for dinner. Soups, salads, and sandwiches are on the lunch menu. Breakfast choices are eggs, bacon or sausage, and either a biscuit or toast. I try to have pancakes or waffles with fruit at least once while folks are here," he said.

"If I helped you with the catering, what did you want me to make?" I asked.

"Well, I'd like for you to make dinners of your choice every night when people are here. You could even use my kitchen if you'd like. Do you have fancy recipes you plan to feature at your restaurant?" he asked in return.

"I like to get creative with my entrées and have hired a chef from New York who also likes to make creative menus." I smiled.

"What's his name?" he asked.

"His name's Gabe. He was driving through Reverence and saw the sign about Southern Thyme Catering Company at Gus's Station. I think he's going to be a great asset to the restaurant, just like Jo Ellen," I said.

"Jo Ellen is a great young lady. Her mother, Bonnie, and grandmother Clara were born and raised outside Reverence on the Rancho del Sol now run by Jo Ellen's uncle, Joe Pete Butler. She was named after her uncle. We continue to call her by both names, but most folks call him Pete. He's a retired major general in the United States Army. He's Clara's youngest son and Bonnie's brother. Clara lost her older son in a terrorist attack overseas several years ago when Pete wajust a boy. We think that's why he enlisted in the army. He rose up in rank rather quickly and we all thought he'd make a career of it, but he received an honorable discharge a year ago and is now back at the ranch taking care of the day-to-day activities.

Clara had a foreman running the ranch, but he had a falling-out with Pete when he returned and then the foreman disappeared without telling anyone where he was going a few months back," Silas remarked.

We were suddenly interrupted by a tall stranger standing inside the door.

"Jones Chancellor was stealing cows off the ranch and selling them to ranchers in Mexico," he said.

"Did he get caught stealing cows? Where is he now?" I asked.

"Good afternoon, Pete. I didn't hear you come in. This is Trinity Taylor, the owner of the new restaurant in town. Jo Ellen might have told you about it." Silas blushed his three shades of red.

"Jo Ellen didn't tell me about it, but Mom did," he said with an unsmiling face.

I stood up to shake Mr. Butler's hand, but he walked past me and sat on the other side of Silas. He looked at me for what seemed like a very long time before saying, "No, the sheriff couldn't find the cows that were stolen. Thanks for asking. It's nice to finally meet you, Trinity. I hope you'll be successful with your restaurant. Reverence needs a quality place to eat." He smirked as he looked at Silas.

"How would you know what I serve here to eat? You've never ordered anything since you've been back." Silas chuckled.

I listened to and watched the two men interact for several minutes before Otis broke up their conversation by saying, "I think we need to let Trinity talk now. She's our guest."

Pete and Silas stopped talking and looked at Otis with respect. He might be slow but he knew how to command attention. I smiled at him and laid my hand over his. "Otis, you are a gentleman and I thank you for letting me join you today for lunch, but now I need to go back into town and meet George. Thanks, Silas, for the scrumptious lunch and for setting up the interview with your friend," I said as I got up and walked to the front door.

"Miss Taylor, may I accompany you to your car?" Pete Butler asked.

"I'd be honored, Mr. Butler." I curtsied.

"Please call me Pete." He smiled.

Silas stayed back to clear the table, but Otis followed us to the car. "Trinity, can you come back tomorrow?" he asked.

"Not tomorrow, I have too many projects on my calendar for the next two weeks, but I will be back soon." I smiled at him.

Pete nodded his farewell as he opened my door. I drove back to town, thinking about my day. One thing was for sure: Pete Butler was a good-looking man!

* * *

Peering through the windshield after driving a few miles, I noticed someone standing in the middle of the road. He was not moving at all. Just like the "man" I thought I saw in the museum last evening, this guy looked like a statute. Surely one of the museum's mannequins couldn't be on Paradise Road.

Why wasn't he trying to walk to the edge of the road? I was going to hit him if he didn't move out of the way, but he didn't budge. At the last minute, I veered to the right to avoid contact. My car hit some loose gravel pieces and I lost control of the wheel. I tried to overcorrect and the car started spinning and heading for the ditch. The last thing I remembered before hitting a boulder on the other side of the ditch was seeing a dark figure in the middle of the road to my left, just standing there as if nothing else was going on around him.

Chapter 3: A Brief Visit to the Mountain View Mercy Hospital

Micha's Mexicana Sauce

1 can diced tomatoes

1 can Ro-Tel tomatoes

2 jalapeños

¼ yellow onion

1 clove garlic

⅛ cup cut fresh cilantro leaves

Juice from 1 lime

30 shakes lemon pepper

⅛ teaspoon salt

⅛ teaspoon dry cilantro

⅛ teaspoon garlic salt

1 tablespoon fresh or dried red thyme

Blend all ingredients in a blender.

"Trinity, can you hear me? Trinity, open your eyes? Squeeze my hand if you can hear me," I heard a voice shouting at me. All I wanted to do was sleep. Why was she yelling?

"Trinity, my name is Zoë. I'm a nurse at Mountain View Mercy Hospital. Please squeeze my hand."

Why was I asleep in a hospital and not in my own bed above Southern Thyme Catering Company?

I slowly opened one eye and then the other. There was a petite brunette smiling down at me.

Turning my head was painful, but I needed to see my surroundings. On my right was a small bedside table with a mounted computer screen above it. To my left was a window with blinds that were shut. I wished they were open so I could see outside.

As if she could read my mind, the nurse walked over to the window and opened the blinds so that I could see the beautiful Arizona sunrise.

"What time is it? How long have I been here?" I asked.

"It's almost seven a.m. You've been here for almost two days. You were in a car accident. You have a broken ankle, several cuts and bruises, and you suffered a nasty bump on your head, which caused a concussion. Do you remember anything about the wreck?" she asked.

"I remember trying to swerve so that I wouldn't hit the man walking down the middle of the road. The last thing I saw was him just standing, not moving at all," I explained.

Zoë raised her eyebrows and then said, "There wasn't anyone else on Paradise Road when the paramedics got the call about your wreck."

"Who called them about my accident? I didn't have time to contact anyone for help," I insisted.

"I don't know how they knew about your predicament. Jarrett, the paramedic who brought you in, could probably give you more information. I'll ask him to come visit you so thatyou can find out more about how you got here," Zoë said as she softly touched my shoulder. "You need to rest. I'll order some breakfast now that you're awake. It's good to see your eyes open. We've had several people admitted in the last few days who haven't woken up yet and we're all perplexed as to why they're in a comatose state. They don't seem to have any injuries."

"Were they in car accidents, too?" I asked.

"No, two were brought in by family members who couldn't get them to wake up at home. One sleeper was in his car outside a restaurant and the other man came in from Reverence like you. I believe he works at the museum in town," she said.

"Is his name Walt?" I asked excitedly.

"I think so, but I'm not really at liberty to give you other patients' names," she said.

Before I could ask her anything else, her paging device beeped on her wrist and she excused herself as she left the room.

* * *

I must have dozed off, because I woke with a start to someone saying my name. “Miss Trinity, my name is Jarrett. I was one of the paramedics who brought you in a couple of days ago. How are you feeling?”

“I’m good and ready to go home. I have a restaurant grand opening just around the corner,” I replied.

“Zoë said you had questions for me. What would you like to know?” He smiled.

“Well, I’m confused about why the man I almost hit wasn’t around when you rescued me. Was he the one that called? Did the person who called identify himself?” I asked.

“Silas Warner was the caller. He was on his way into town when he saw your car upside down and called for help. The dispatcher said he was in tears when he called and said we needed to hurry and get you to the hospital. He even told her he would hold all of us personally responsible if something serious happened to you.” He chuckled.

“He was there when we arrived, holding your hand and praying that you’d be okay. There wasn’t anyone else around. The only person who lives in the area is Old Man Amos. He has lived alone since his wife died a few years back. His house is down a gravel road right by where we rescued you," he continued.

I asked if he'd seen anything out of the ordinary lately when helping people that he brought to the hospital.

"As a matter of fact, I have transported several people in a comatose state within the span of a few days, and we're calling them sleepers. I was on my way to meet with my supervisor to report this very fact when I was asked to come see you. We need advice from the National Disease Control Board as to what we could be dealing with here."

As he was explaining this, the door opened to my room and I saw Becca Ellis, the museum curator.

"Becca, come on in. It's great to see you," I exclaimed.

"Hi, Trinity. I thought I'd check on you to see how you're doing and when you'll be well enough to go home," Becca said.

"I'm fine. I should go home today or early tomorrow morning. Thanks so much for coming," I said.

"I came to visit with you and to see about Walt. He's here, too. Unfortunately, he's in a coma and no one knows why." She sighed.

"Have you talked with his family to ask what they know?" I asked.

"Walt doesn't have any family around. My understanding is the hospital is calling in his next of kin from New Mexico. Since I'm not related to him the nurse on duty wouldn't tell me much," Becca replied.

"Excuse me, Becca. Where are my manners? Jarrett, this is my new friend, Becca. He's the paramedic who brought me to the hospital for treatment," I explained, motioning to the man standing beside my bed.

"Hello, Becca. I've heard about you. You're the one in charge of the museum in Reverence, right?" Jarrett said.

"Yes, I am. Have you visited the museum?" she asked.

"No, but I couldn't help overhearing you talk about Walt. I brought him in a couple of days ago. He and I met a few weeks back in the Twinkle City Laundromat in town and he told me he worked for you," Jarrett said.

"Do you have any idea what happened to him? Did he say anything about feeling bad when you met him?" Becca asked.

"No, ma'am. I don't. Something strange is going on around here. We need help from experts as to what we are supposed to do with Walt and others like him," he said as he hung his head.

"There are others?" Becca gasped.

"Yes, ma'am, but I've already said too much. Please excuse me, ladies. I need to get back to work," Jarrett said as he turned and walked out the door.

"Trinity, I have goosebumps on my arms. What's happening?" she said.

"I don't know and it's upsetting to say the least. I need to get home to open the restaurant. Call me tomorrow. We have a lot to talk about," I replied.

Becca nodded and then left. Everything was quiet in the hospital. I laid my head back on the pillow, closed my eyes, and prayed that God would lift those up affected by whatever was going on. How many more people would fall ill to the strange happenings in and around Reverence?

Chapter 4: The Southern Thyme Catering Company Grand Opening Hitch and the Donkey Parade

Kim's Salsa

1 large can whole peeled tomatoes
1 can fire-roasted tomatoes
1 onion
2 jalapeños
1 serrano
3 cloves garlic
1 bunch cilantro, tops only
1 cluster fresh Spanish thyme leaves
Pepper to taste, preferably coarse-ground
Mix all ingredients in blender.

"Mom, it's so good to hear your voice!" I said over the phone as the tears trickled down my face. She could tell that something was wrong even though she couldn't see me. I shut off the camera device so my disposition wouldn't be visible on the screen; however, I could never keep anything from my mother. She knew something was wrong right away.

"Trinity, what's happened?"

"Do you want me to start with the latest episode first?" I asked.

"I want you to tell me everything that is going on with you," she replied.

"I should have called before now, but you would've stopped what you're doing and come to Reverence." I chuckled nervously.

"Trinity Grace Taylor, start talking," she commanded.

"I just got out of the Mountain View Mercy Hospital between here and Willcox. Before you get on to me for not calling from the hospital, let me tell you the reason I waited to call." I sighed before telling her about the "man" in the road, the wreck, and my broken ankle.

"Trinity, I think I need to be there for you. You can't open the restaurant without help," Mom said.

"How about sending Grandma Cora? She's still as spry as ever and I think she would love to be a part of the grand opening," I responded.

"I wish I could be there too, but with all that's going on around here, you're right. It would be difficult to get away. Your grandmother will be on cloud nine when she knows she gets to be with you and help boss everyone around." Mom laughed.

"With her help, I know it's going to be a huge success," I said.

* * *

Today was the grand opening for Southern Thyme Catering Company. Grandma Cora had been such a godsend. She had run Jean and Joe's Place, the family restaurant in Texas, for many years before retiring, so her expertise went a long way when we planned our big day. The staff had been great. Becca brought an early American café display from the museum for the front foyer and Jo Ellen helped with the restaurant decorations. She created two "Food Feature" boards so that people could choose what they wanted to eat. Her "Salsa on the Side" choices were on a miniature easel at each table, with another one for the center of the counter. We wanted to sponsor a salsa contest in conjunction with the grand opening but decided to postpone it to another time due to the car accident.

I'd envisioned a perfect day. Alas, no day was really ever really perfect. This one would go down in the history books as one of the most unique grand openings of all time.

"Trinity, are you ready for me to open the front doors, or do you want to be the one who greets the people already in line on the porch?" Jo Ellen asked.

"You can open them. I plan to mingle as people are seated and explain the 'Food Feature' boards, as well as the menus," I replied.

Grandma Cora opted to stay in the kitchen so that she could help Chef Gabe organize the kitchen and the food orders. I remember closing my eyes and thanking God for a beautiful sunshiny day as I was listening to one of the classic songs I'd relabeled on the old jukebox to fit the theme of the restaurant: "Thyme Is on My Side" by the Rolling Stones. The townspeople began pouring in through the front door.

It was heartwarming to see so many of the community members taking time in their busy day to attend this special occasion. Becca came in with Saydi, glancing over at the display they'd brought over. They turned and smiled at me before finding a table. Lois Tull, owner of Twinkle City Laundromat, walked past me with her eyes fixed on something ahead.

"Lois, it's wonderful to have you here today," I said, smiling.

She didn't acknowledge my greeting. She continued to walk to the counter, eyes unblinking, but instead of sitting on one of the stools, she just stood there staring at who knew what.

Before I could ask her if anything was wrong, Silas was in front of me. "Trinity, have you seen Otis?" he asked.

"Not yet. Didn't he ride into town with you?" I asked.

"He said he'd be coming in our old truck. He told me he had a surprise for you and didn't want me to spoil it." He chuckled.

"Maybe he'll show up soon and reveal his special gift."

Suddenly I heard not one, but multiple dishes breaking in the kitchen. Everyone froze in their tracks as they peered over the counter, trying to sneak a peek at what was causing all the commotion. I ran to the kitchen like I was running the hundred-meter dash. Just as I got inside the swinging doors, I was shoved to the left as a large furry animal lumbered past me. It was a good thing I fell on my rump and stayed on the floor, because I watched four smaller furry critters follow the bigger one into the dining area. Close behind them was Otis, hollering, "Frosty, stop!"

The entire train of donkeys disappeared out the front door almost as quickly as they'd entered the building. Gabe pulled me up and asked if I was all right. I didn't want to go out into the dining area, but I knew I had to see what damage had occurred. Ironically, no one was hurt. Jo Ellen had ushered the customers to their seats as the donkeys ran through the restaurant.

I decided it best to say something to break the tension along with the dishes. "Now that I have your attention, how would you like apple pie à la mode on the house?" Everyone cheered even though I could see many of our patrons had fear written all over their faces.

Instead of being afraid, Grandma Cora was standing inside the swinging doors laughing so hard she was doubled over.

"Trinity, this incident reminds me of the day your grandpa and I got married," she said as she tried to catch her breath.

"Mr. Johnson's prize hog crashed our wedding reception. My new husband's cousin Sally Jane was knocked over and fell face-first into his groom's cake. It was the second time Sally Jane blamed me for ruining her dress from Paris. I'll save that first story for another time." She continued laughing.

* * *

At the end of the day, Jo Ellen ordered me to sit down while she finished sweeping the floor. I laid my head on the table briefly. Before long I felt someone tap my shoulder.

"Trinity, I'm so sorry that Frosty and her friends ruined your grand opening," Otis sighed. "I wanted you to see my mini burros—Cici, Pal, Fig, and Valentine. You might have noticed Valentine at the end of the line. She has a heart-shaped spot on her charcoal head. A lot of people call them burritos, but not the kind that's okay to be in a restaurant."

"That's funny, Otis. I like their names. You don't have to apologize. No one was hurt and we still had a successful event. How did your animals get loose?"

He stared at me for a moment, thinking about my comments, then said, "The trailer door was open because I was going to lead them out one by one to meet you. I forgot this was your big opening day. Instead of cheering you up after being in your accident, I wrecked your special day. Will you forgive me?" Otis bent down to look at me face to face.

"How would you like to have some apple pie à la mode?" I smiled.

"Does that mean I'm forgiven? Can I just have the apple pie with ice cream on top instead?" he asked.

"Yes and yes!" I laughed.

* * *

The next morning, Jo Ellen came blaring through the front door. Her face looked as pale as the full moon from the night before.

"Trinity, Lois Tull was found unconscious in her laundromat this morning when her first customer came in to do laundry. Apparently she lay on the floor behind her counter all night according to Jarrett. He was the one who took her to the hospital. Isn't he the paramedic who took you to Mountain View Mercy Hospital?" she asked."He's the one. I think he's been on call each time someone has been found unconscious," I replied.

"By the way, my uncle Pete sent the bouquet on the counter for our special day. With all the commotion, I forgot to tell you about it," Jo Ellen said before walking into the kitchen.

I strolled over to relish the fragrance of the fresh-cut flowers and noticed a card attached. It read, *Trinity, may your grand opening go smoothly without any hitches. Wish I could be there! Pete.*

I sighed as I reread his message. Reverence was indeed experiencing many hitches lately.

It was obvious that others would be affected by the unknown sickness if we didn't contact someone to help us solve this ongoing mystery.

Chapter 5: It's the Thyme

Robin's Salsa
3 cups diced variety tomatoes
½ cup diced Anaheim pepper
½ cup diced green onion
¼ cup diced jalapeño, including seeds
3 tablespoons chopped cilantro
½ teaspoon garlic powder
1 teaspoon onion powder
½ teaspoon cumin
2 tablespoons fresh lime juice
1 tablespoon English thyme
1 teaspoon kosher salt
½ teaspoon ground black pepper
Add to bowl and gently mix together.

"Trinity, I just met the nicest group of ladies," Grandma Cora said as she burst through the kitchen doors.

"You amaze me how vibrant you are, especially in the morning." I smiled.

"I have always loved mornings. Your friend who is ill, Lois, is a member of the Reverence Bridge Club. Her bridge partners said they want to do something to pay her medical bills. I suggested we donate the salsa-contest entry fees to her family. I hope that's okay with you since I already offered." She chuckled. Before I could answer, she continued with her story. "They also asked me to join them for their next bridge game. Did you know I used to play once a week back in Truway?"

"No, I didn't, but in answer to your first question, I love the idea of donating the entryfee money to Lois's family. And we could play bingo for one dollar a card, giving the other affected community members the proceeds. Everyone can play while the judges are tasting the salsas. The salsa winners will get the privilege of being on our featured boards for an entire week. The bingo champions will receive the salsas entered as prizes. We'll call the event *Salsa Thyme Extravaganza!* What do you think?" I asked.

"Great ideas. I'll call my new friends and let them know the plan," Grandma Cora exclaimed.

* * *

The next morning the Reverence Bridge Club members came in for coffee and one of their games. My exuberant grandmother was joined by her new friends--Billye, Jimmie, and Suzanne. It was so much fun listening to their stories.

Billye told us about Lois's love for flag dancing, which she did on Sunday mornings at the local non-denominational church. Grandma Cora told the women about her twin, Cara, who lived in New Mexico. Cara had lived a long life on the Las Bonitas Ranch even though she had Marfan's syndrome, a genetic disorder affecting the connective tissue in the human body. Some people suffered with heart problems, but Cara had issues with loose joints, a curved spine, and poor eyesight.She was one of the first Marfan's patients to get artificial lenses, but as she aged, her eyesight failed. She lost her husband, Glen, who also had Marfan's, in 2020. Cara died in 2032.

The ladies couldn't believe that Grandma was ninety-six years old. She blushed at the comment and then told them about Lottie, the aunt who raised her, and how she lived to be one hundred and six. Before long her friends were laughing so hard they were unable to catch their breath as she shared the story about how she ruined her husband's cousin's FIRST dress from Paris:

"When Cara and I went to a private all-girls' school, we had to work in the cafeteria to pay for our tuition. One night we were supposed to serve ice-cream sundaes to a group of sorority girls and their guests, the boys from a private school across town.

Of course, I wanted to hurry up and finish serving so that I could have my own ice-cream sundae. Therefore, I decided to put twice as many parfaits on the tray as instructed. As a result, I tipped the tray over and spilled ice cream and chocolate sauce all over the president of the sorority, Sally Jane Nelson. She was Austin Chilacothe's cousin, a boy that I went to school with, who eventually became my husband and Trinity's grandfather."

I had never heard the stories about the dresses from Paris. Hearing them the past two days had endeared my grandmother to me even more. Where would we be without stories passed on to us from our parents and grandparents?

* * *

The bell above the front door rang. I expected to see Otis come in for his daily breakfast visit, but instead I was surprised to see Pete stride in.

"Howdy, Trinity. It's good to see you walking around without crutches. I envisioned you taking it easy while your restaurant employees wait on the customers." He grinned.

"Not on your life. I want to serve our patrons, too, even if it takes longer to get around. What brings you in today?" I asked, smiling.

"I'm on my way to visit with Colonel Jet Heath, who's meeting me at Whispering Breeze Canyon about twenty-five miles north of here. He wants me to head up an army investigation concerning a truck that's gone missing and has been missing for a while," he remarked while choosing a barstool at the counter.

"Missing truck? Is the driver missing too?" I asked.

"He is. He radioed the army base an hour before his truck went off the grid. He told the dispatcher that he was feeling lightheaded and didn't think he could make it all the way to the base. An hour later, he and the truck just disappeared. The last GPS signal was outside the entrance to the canyon. That's why I'm meeting the colonel there," Pete answered.

"Strange that both have vanished. If the driver wrecked, the truck should be somewhere obvious even if the driver wandered off. Do you think he might be another coma victim?" I asked.

"Could be. Colonel Heath didn't confide in me about what was being transported and by whom. If I take over the investigation, the government will have to trust me with more information," he said.

Pete ordered breakfast and offered to enter his own salsa recipe into our contest. I thanked him for the beautiful bouquet of flowers and left him to eat in peace while I checked on the ladies.

The next thing I knew the front bell was ringing again. Pete was leaving, but before going out the door, he turned, made eye contact, and tipped his cowboy hat in my direction.

I blushed and waved, hoping he'd return soon from the canyon with more news about the truck and the driver.

* * *

Otis visited later than usual. Breakfast time was officially over, but I knew he'd want eggs and a pancake. Sure enough, that was what he ordered. While he waited for his food, he sat and stared into space. It scared me for a moment because that was what I had seen Lois doing when she was here for the grand opening.

"Otis, are you okay?" I asked.

"Yes, Trinity. I was just thinking about Walt, Lois, and the others who are still sleeping at the hospital. Silas told me Mel is sick and on his way to Mercy. He also told me they found Old Man Amos sitting on a bale of hay in his barn just staring, so they took him to the hospital, too. That's why I'm late for my visit today. I don't know if they're awake or not. Do you want to hear my theory about who's asleep and who's not?" Otis asked.

"Of course. Tell me what you think is going on. I'm all ears," I said as I touched his arm.

Otis looked at the left side of my face, then the right, before he began talking. It dawned on me that he was making sure I only had two ears. He took everything literally.

"It's the thyme," he said as he looked around to see who might be listening.

"What do you mean 'it's the time'? Time for what?" I asked.

"Not 'time,' 'thyme,'" he emphasized. "You know, the stuff you put into your salsas and other recipes. People who eat thyme aren't sleeping too much. People who don't like thyme are the ones in the hospital," he said.

"How do you know who likes thyme and who doesn't?" I asked with my eyebrows raised.

He moved in closer and whispered, "Lois and Walt told me they don't eat thyme. Lois said it makes her break out into a rash. Walt admitted that he doesn't like the taste. We talked about it one day when I was in town at the laundromat. So I believe it's the thyme that's keeping us upright." He stood to illustrate his point before sitting back down.

Wow! It sounded incredible, but could it be true? Otis did have an uncanny talent for observing other people. When he was in a crowd he would sit back and stay quiet while listening to all the talk around him. It almost seemed as if he was invisible in a room filled with chatter. Maybe that was how he'd become so astute. Or maybe it was God's gift to him as a part of his learning differences. Either way, there was more to Otis Warner than most folks realized.

As I was pondering what Otis had said, I looked up and saw that he was leaving the restaurant. He turned and met my bewildered gaze.

"Trinity, it's the thyme!" he bellowed.

Even if Otis's theory was accurate, how did we revive our friends?

* * *

Pete stopped back by the restaurant before going home later that evening. I was about to lock the front door and head upstairs to bed when I heard him knock on the door.

"Trinity, it's me, Pete Butler. Do you have time to talk to me over a cup of coffee?"

"It'll keep me up all night, but I'll drink water while you sip your brew. I'm curious to hear what you found out," I said as I opened the door.

Pete repeated the events at Whispering Breeze Canyon, but not before he made me promise to keep everything he told me in the strictest confidence. I was surprised he wanted to confide in me.

He met with Colonel Heath, who told him that the last GPS signal they had received was at the entrance to the canyon; however, there wasn't any evidence of a truck or a driver anywhere around. They were totally baffled.

Pete asked what was being transported on the truck. At first, the colonel hesitated to say, but then he realized that if they needed Pete's help locating the truck and driver, he would have to know what was being transported.

"Well, what was it?" I asked.

Pete sighed and said, "Barrels of a toxic substance that were supposed to show up at the Arizona Army Base. Only certified personnel knew about the mission. The security level in DC was raised to level four a few months back. The substance was created in a lab there and was being sent to the remote Arizona lab for further tests. The government didn't know what they were going to do with the barrels in the long run. The immediate plan is to find the truck and driver and make sure everyone is safe."

"Safe?" I asked.

"Yes. If the substance is removed from the barrels without people wearing proper hazmat gear to open them, there's no telling what could happen. So either the driver wrecked the truck or someone intercepted it before reaching the Arizona base. Since there's no sign of a wreck, we have to assume that someone stopped the truck before entering the canyon. The driver was either on the take or he was kidnapped, maybe even killed," Pete said with a look of concern.

"I have faith in you! You'll be able to solve the mystery eventually," I encouraged.

"Thanks for believing in me. As I was traveling back after taking pictures of the area and gathering some dirt samples, I started thinking about the people who have fallen ill for no apparent reason. Could the toxic substance in the barrels have caused their illness? Who would want to steal the barrels and why?" Pete said as he stood up to leave.

Chapter 6: Whispering Breeze Canyon and the Salsa Thyme Extravaganza

Monica's Sassy Salsa Recipe
6 jalapeños
2 peeled tomatoes
1 avocado
1 tablespoon cilantro
1 small onion
1 teaspoon Spanish thyme
½ cup water
Mix all ingredients in a blender. Enjoy!

Pete dropped by again for breakfast and officially entered the salsa contest. We posted flyers all over town and put an ad in the local paper about the Salsa Thyme Extravaganza. The event would take place at the end of the week, and we were excited about all the buzz surrounding it. Six other community members had fallen ill and were unresponsive, so we needed to help the families as much as we could. The contest was like a small ray of hope for Reverence, even if no one woke up.

Becca and I planned to take a trip to the hospital to see what the administrators had found out from the National Infectious Disease experts.

"Pete, Becca and I are going to the hospital later today to talk to the staff about what might be going on," I said as I poured him a cup of coffee.

"That's great, but I was going to ask you to take a ride out to the canyon with me if you can break away for a spell," he said.

"Let me talk to Jo Ellen about running the show here and then I'll go with you and meet Becca at the hospital this afternoon," I replied.

That afternoon while riding out to the canyon, I realized that I hadn't told Pete about Otis's thyme theory.

"Otis seems to think that the 'sleepers' who are 'sleeping,' as he calls it, are ones who don't eat thyme," I said.

"Are you saying that an herb is a cure?" he asked in an exasperated voice.

"I'm not saying that's what I think. It's Otis's idea; however, he has researched who eats thyme and who doesn't. I think it's worth mentioning to the hospital administrators. It won't hurt to have them talk it over with the disease board," I said.

"No, I guess not, but it seems rather bizarre to think an herb could keep people from falling asleep," he said.

Before I could say anything more, I noticed a sign up ahead that read *Whispering Breeze Canyon Road, next exit.*

We drove in silence for a few minutes. The stress of the last few weeks' events was catching up with all of us. Pete was the first to break the silence after stopping the truck.

"We're here, but don't get out until you put this on," he said as he handed me a gas mask.

"Did you wear one of these when you visited Colonel Heath?" I asked.

"No, but I should have. I'm not taking any chances, especially with you in tow," he replied.

I took the mask and placed the strap over my head, glancing at myself in his rearview mirror. Staring back at me was what looked like an alien from outer space. If Otis's theory was correct I didn't need the mask, but I decided to wear it for Pete's sake. (No pun intended.)

"Trinity, help me look for signs—footprints, objects that don't belong, or anything you think seems important to note about the area," Pete instructed.

At first all I saw was red clay dirt when I looked around. No animal or human prints were visible. Just when I was thinking that the search was futile, I saw a shiny object to my right just beyond a cactus plant. I walked over and plucked it from the dirt, careful not to touch the spines protruding from the plant.

"Pete, I found something interesting," I said.

I handed him what appeared to be a boot tip. Grandpa Austin had worn boot tips for special occasions in Truway. This silver relic resembled one of his tips.

"What is it?" he asked.

"It's a boot tip. Cowboys wear them on the toes of their boots for special occasions. Don't you own some?" I asked.

"No, but I've seen these on several cowboys in the past. I knew you'd be an asset to this investigation." He smiled.

"Thanks! Now all we have to do is figure out who this one belongs to." I chuckled.

Pete put the tip into his shirt pocket and we continued our search for other helpful clues.

"Wait! Don't take another step. What's that in front of you?" he asked excitedly.

Looking down, I saw another shiny object. I picked it up and rotated it in the palm of my hand.

"I don't know what this is," I said.

"I've seen that before," he said. "It's a laser cufflink. It's used to keep people from bumping into things at night. There should be a button under the stone. Do you feel it?" he asked.

I ran my fingers underneath the scarlet stone and found the button he was talking about.

"Yes, I feel it," I said.

"Push it in and hold it for a few seconds," he said.

All of a sudden, a dark red light not only illuminated the stone, but projected a ray of red light for several feet.

"Wow, this is so cool. I've never seen one of these. How did you know what it was?" I asked.

"The man who used to work for us on the ranch saved a month's wages to get a pair of these. He showed them to everyone just before I let him go," Pete replied with a stern look on his face.

"What was his name?" I asked.

"Jones Chancellor. What would he be doing way out here? I have a suspicious feeling that he's involved in this mess somehow," Pete replied.

He put the cufflink in his other shirt pocket and we continued to survey the land again.

We didn't find anything else, not even a footprint, which was strange since we knew one or more people had to have been in the vicinity. At least we had something to investigate further.

* * *

I met Becca at the hospital as planned. We were escorted to the director's office, where the National

Infectious Disease Board had set up headquarters. The count had risen to sixty-four patients who had fallen comatose countywide. At the rate the sick people were arriving, the hospital would run out of beds soon.

"Thank you for agreeing to meet with us and telling us the current number of patients. What are you going to do when there are no more rooms available?" Becca asked.

"We're on the lookout for a nearby place that could act as an overflow hospital. Neither one of you has any ideas where we could go, do you?" the hospital director asked.

I thought about all the places I'd toured lately. The Oasis Club Resort popped into my head.

"I do!" I said excitedly. "Do you know Silas Warner, the owner of the Oasis Club Resort?" I asked.

"Yes, I met him when he came in with his brother several weeks ago," he answered.

"I think you should call him and ask him about the possibility of turning his bunkhouses and private rooms into hospital rooms. We could even make his restaurant available for visitors and staff members," I said.

The director thanked me for the idea and said he would follow up with Silas. I planned to call Silas myself when I returned and offer to oversee the kitchen and dining area. Jo Ellen and Gabe could run the restaurant in Reverence for a short period of time.

Before we left I talked to the disease board personnel about Otis's thyme theory. They said they'd give it some thought and do a little research and then get back with me.

If I wanted to supervise the move to the Oasis and host the Salsa Thyme Extravaganza, I needed to be able to wear not one but two walking shoes. Maybe I could make an appointment to see my doctor while here to see if it would be possible to get rid of this special boot.

* * *

I returned to the restaurant before sundown and encountered Jo Ellen getting ready for our big extravaganza.

"Trinity, we have eleven salsas entered into the contest. All of the contestants agreed to put thyme in their recipes, as you requested. It's going to be a fabulous event," she said.

"I hope so. There are so many families who need our help," I replied.

What a night! All of the Reverence community members came out to support the Salsa Thyme. Not only did local folks attend, but people from Willcox and the other surrounding towns came, too. Bingo was a hit. Otis was our caller. He made it so fun with his loud auctioneer-type voice.

"B2. The number is B2, ladies and gentlemen," he boomed. He enunciated so clearly each time he picked up a ball from the rolling cage. When someone yelled "Bingo," he would say, "Hold your cards and markers, please. We may have a winner."

Grandma Cora asked if she could announce the winner of the salsa contest. How could I say no to her? She would be going back to Texas in a couple of days. I knew I would miss her so much. She'd helped to organize the entire evening, so she deserved the honor of recognizing the salsa champions.

While the judges were tallying their scores, we played old songs on our jukebox—"Time Is on My Side," "I've Had the Time of My Life," "Time Stands Still," "Old Time Rock and Roll," "Time After Time," and "Time of the Season." We painted the titles on signs and taped them on each wall. We replaced the word "time" with "thyme" to go with our theme. I was surprised how many people knew these classic songs from the past. Otis knew all the lyrics to every song.

"I sing in my room every day after chores," he told me, grinning. His attention to detail never ceased to amaze me.

The coolest part of the night was seeing the holograms that Gabe had programmed into the computer wall monitor. Watching the Zombies dance around the stage singing "Time of the Season" was so realistic. It was like the band members were actually in the room.

Grandma Cora grabbed the microphone and announced the salsa winners. "Third place goes to Pete Butler for his 'Pete's Hot Sauce.' Second place is awarded to 'Deborah's A Thyme for Peaches,' and the first-place champion is...drumroll, please...'Tres Amigas Avocado-Cilantro Sauce'!" she exclaimed, and started clapping as soon as she said the first-place winners' names.

It was a good thing we hadn't let her judge the winning salsas, because the Tres Amigas were her friends—Billye, Jimmie, and Suzanne. Gabe, Jo Ellen, Becca, and Saydi were the judges, so we had them also take a bow at the end of the announcement.

Before everyone headed out for the evening, I hugged Otis and said, "You really are something!"

"Thanks, Trinity. You haven't seen anything yet. I'm going to help you and Pete figure out who's responsible for the missing truck, driver, and barrels. I know for a fact that the missing items and driver are linked to our sleeping friends. We just have to connect the motive to the crimes and then we'll find our bad guy," he said in a hushed voice.

How did he know about the missing army details? Did he overhear Pete and me talking?

What motive could anyone have to hurt people in and around Reverence? Only "thyme" would tell.

Chapter 7: Oasis Club & Resort Hospital

Theresa's Salsa

4 cups tomatoes, skinned and chopped
1 medium onion
2 mild jalapeños, seeded
2 medium jalapeños, seeded
1 teaspoon honey
½ teaspoon cumin
1 clove garlic
½ teaspoon salt
½ teaspoon orange thyme
Small handful cilantro

In blender, pulse 1 cup of tomatoes and other ingredients, except cilantro, until fine. Then blend the remaining 3 cups of tomatoes and cilantro.

Silas surprised me with an early call the next morning.

"Trinity, the Mountain View Mercy Hospital director called and asked if his staff could set up a meeting with me to explore the possibility of making the Oasis Club Resort an overflow hospital."

"What did you tell him?" I asked.

"I told him only if I can talk Trinity Taylor into running the kitchen and dining area." He chuckled.

"Actually, I gave him the idea of contacting you. I planned to call you to see if you'd like for me to help organize the transition," I said.

"It's good to know we're on the same page. I'll contact you later with the details," he said.

He called the next morning to let me know we only had three days to get the resort ready for business. Ironically, Brother Dan from the non-denominational church came into Southern Thyme for breakfast, and when I told him about the overflow hospital he offered to help me do an inventory of what was in stock and what needed to be ordered at the new site.

"Trinity, I truly believe that God is asking me to assist you. I used to work in the dormitory kitchen when I was attending the seminary in Tucson," he said.

"Thanks, Brother Dan. Your involvement is so appreciated," I replied.

He not only made a list of what was available and what we needed to order, but also planned to have a special day each week for family members to meet with him at breakfast to talk about their loved ones and then pray for their healing.

* * *

Everyone at Southern Thyme Catering Company pitched in to make the transition run smoothly.

I had doubted that even with the staff's help we would be able to move into the resort on the designated day, but we did.

Otis met us in the driveway, smiling and waving as our train of vehicles came to a halt just outside the back door to the kitchen.

"I've been up since midnight sitting on the front porch. Today is a special day. I'm here to help you move your equipment inside. Silas will help, too, but right now he's in a meeting with the hospital people," he said as he opened my car door.

"Thanks. We'll gladly let you help unpack with us," I said as I reached up to hug his neck.

"Trinity, now that you will be here every day for a while, let's talk about the clues of the sleeper mystery," Otis said.

"What clues are you referring to?" I asked.

"Well, I know you and Pete found something when you visited Whispering Breeze Canyon. I just don't know what," he replied.

"Who told you we found clues?" I asked, but made sure to smile so he wouldn't think I was angry.

"No one told me, but when you returned from your trip I saw Pete pat both of his shirt pockets when he dropped you off. He was looking at you in a special way so I knew you two had a secret between you," he said as he smiled back at me.

Otis's knack for noticing things was uncanny. I believed that people thought he was daydreaming most of the time and didn't realize how much he was soaking up when listening to others' conversations or watching their body language.

"Otis, your keen observations are truly a gift," I remarked.

"Thanks. So what did you find?" he asked excitedly.

"I can't reveal any information, but I will be more than happy to sit with you on the porch each evening to discuss 'what ifs.' You do the talking and I'll listen. How does that sound?" I asked.

He showed me his "thumbs up" sign as he left to unload the car.

* * *

Otis and I didn't meet on the porch for the first three days. We were so busy setting things up that there wasn't time in the day to say anything to one another other than "I hope you are having a great day." Finally, on our fourth day of operation, Otis approached me and said, "Did you and Pete visit the Lost Canyon Mine yet?"

"No, I didn't know there was such a place. Do you know where it is?" I asked.

"My dad took us there when it was still in existence over fifty years ago, but I think the mining company took down the sign when they had their last cave-in forty years ago. Several of the miners died from suffocation so they decided to shut the mine down for good. I forgot about it until I heard Silas talking with someone on the phone about it. Whoever he was talking to asked Silas if he knew where it was located," he said.

I was going to ask Otis more about Silas's phone call, but Brother Dan interrupted our conversation. "Trinity, do you have a few moments to talk with me?"

"Sure. Otis, let's meet this evening and talk more about the mine," I said, and then turned toward Brother Dan. "Do you want to grab a cup of coffee or tea and sit by the windows in the dining room?"

"Tea with honey sounds heavenly," he said.

"What's up?" I asked after handing him his cup of tea.

"I have some exciting news. Walt squeezed Becca's hand yesterday. She tried to find you and let you know, but you'd driven into town to get more supplies when it happened. She saw me on her way out and asked me to relay the story," exclaimed Brother Dan.

"She was sitting by Walt's bedside, rubbing his hand. She always talked to him about news from the museum. Yesterday, she was telling him how much everyone missed him and how she'd be glad when he woke up and returned to work. As she stood up to leave he grabbed her hand and squeezed it as hard as he could. She said it even hurt, but just as quickly as he grabbed her he had let go. She bent down to peer into his face and asked him to squeeze again, but he didn't respond. She rushed into the hallway and snagged one of the nurses, who immediately went into the room with her. The nurse noted the episode on his digital chart, but she couldn't see anything different in his vital signs on the screen."

Walt, Lois, and others who were some of the first "sleepers" were transferred to the resort, since it was closer to Reverence than the hospital. I looked in on them most every day, but not yesterday. I hoped the staff could go back and research his computer scan report to see if his heartbeat had changed when squeezing Becca's hand. What a breakthrough!

* * *

Once again, Otis and I were unable to talk. I was on my way to the front porch when I saw not one but many staff members running down the hallway.

"What's going on?" I asked Zoë.

"We got a stat page to go to room thirteen," she told me.

I knew whose room that was. It was Lois's room.

I followed everyone through the door. Trying not to interfere with the staff's instructions, I peered around the last nurse's head and saw that Lois had her eyes open and was attempting to lift her head.

I heard Zoë buzz the doctor on call. "The patient in room thirteen is apparently awake. Please get here as soon as possible to examine her."

Before I could ask someone what they thought was happening, I overheard two staff members talking. "It's got to be the thyme extract that the doctors ordered for the initial six patients. Lois Hull is the second person to respond to stimuli in the last twenty-four hours."

What thyme extract? The disease board director had said he'd get back to me about Otis's theory. Apparently the board had not only listened, but also directed the lab staff to develop some type of serum to counteract whatever was causing the infected victims to sleep.

I needed to set up another meeting with the hospital director and ask questions about what might be happening. It was imperative for me to tell Otis the news and ask him why the Lost Canyon Mine was somewhere we needed to visit

I truly believed that Otis was the key to unraveling this whole mess. How long it would take was anyone's guess.

Oasis Club
Resort
Reverence
Hospital

Chapter 8: The Interview and Search for More Clues

Salgado's Salsa
3 parts Roma tomatoes
2 parts white onion
1 part jalapeño
4–5 tablespoons minced garlic
2 tablespoons Himalayan salt
1 bunch cilantro
¼ teaspoon white thyme

Dice the tomatoes, onion, and peppers. Use the whole pepper, including seeds. Add salt, garlic, cilantro, and thyme to taste. Mix and refrigerate. Enjoy!

Otis and I finally met the evening after Lois opened her eyes. Unfortunately, she didn't stay awake long. She closed her eyes and went back to sleep only seconds after she attempted to raise her head.

Otis was beyond excited when I told him about the conversation I'd overheard regarding the thyme extract.

"I told you, Trinity. The thyme is the answer to our problems," he said.

"I agree, but until we locate the root of the problem, the thyme can't totally fix our friends and others affected by the unknown culprit," I said.

"Please tell me what you and Pete found in Whispering Breeze Canyon," he pleaded.

I hesitated because Pete had asked me to keep the items we found quiet. I was sworn to secrecy.

"Did you find something he thinks might belong to Jones Chancellor?" he asked.

"Why do you think that?"

"I overheard Verda Mae talking to Jo Ellen in the restaurant the other day."

"Who's Verda Mae?"

"She's Jones's girlfriend."

"What did you hear her say?" I asked.

"She told Jo Ellen that he'd stood her up again. She also told her how he'd been acting strangely the last time she'd seen him. He was leaving town and told her he'd return in a few days and they'd celebrate something he'd found that would not only make him rich, but would put Reverence on the map."

"Did he come back to town?" I asked, even though I knew what Otis would say next.

"No. She can't find him. Not only did he not show up for their date, but he's not answering his phone and no one he is associated with knows why he hasn't returned."

"I can't tell you what we found, but I can let you know that it's probably a good idea to find out where Jones Chancellor disappeared to."

"Enough said. I believe he's caught up in this mystery. If we find him, we'll find out how he's involved. I'll introduce you to Verda Mae. Getting her to tell us exactly what Jones told her before he disappeared might help us locate him," he said as he walked down the steps and headed toward Frosty's stall. Every morning and evening he gave hay to Frosty and his new mini burros, AKA burritos.

Watching the sun set over the mountains filled me with a hope that tomorrow would be a better day.

* * *

Verda Mae called the next morning and asked if we could meet outside of town. I invited her to the resort, but she declined. She asked, "Do you know where the Reverence rest stop is?"

"I do. We can catch up at three this afternoon if that works for you," I said. She agreed. It was exciting to know she might be able to shed some more light onto what was happening to cause so many people to "sleep."

* * *

When I pulled up to the picnic pavilion at the rest stop, a lanky young girl with spiky white hair stepped out of her vehicle. She didn't acknowledge me when I got out of my Jeep. She walked toward one of the tables, sat down, and looked around as if she thought someone might be watching us.

"Are you Verda Mae?" I asked as I took a seat across from her.

"Yes, I am. You're Trinity Taylor. I've eaten in your restaurant several times. Jo Ellen pointed you out to me once. By the way, your Southern thyme chicken is my favorite entrée. Your place is a good addition to Reverence. I can't stay long. I'm on my way out of town," she said.

"Are you going to meet Jones somewhere?" I asked.

"No, I still don't know where he is. No sooner had I agreed to meet with you about his disappearance than an army colonel came to my trailer and asked to speak to me," she said as she continued to suspiciously look around the rest area.

"Did you tell him about your last conversation with Jones?"

"No, I told him I didn't know where Jones was, which is true, but I also told him I'd not spoken with him in over a month."

"Why did you tell him that?"

"I don't know. I don't want to get involved with the military. I had a cousin who went AWOL a few years back and we never heard from him again. I'm going to leave town and stay with my cousin in Willcox for a while. I'm scared to be here right now. It sounds like Jones has gotten himself into something dangerous and I don't want to end up missing, too," she said as she sighed heavily.

"Thanks for agreeing to talk to me even though you're frightened. We need to find Jones as soon as possible. He may have important information about what's going on. The quicker we find him, the quicker we might be able to figure out how we can help our friends who are sick."

"Do you really think he's behind what's happening to all the people who are in the hospital?" she asked.

"I don't know if he's behind the reason they are sick, but I do think he might know who is," I replied.

"If he calls, you'll be the first to know," she said as she got up and walked to her car.

* * *

That evening I had dinner with Pete at the restaurant. I filled him in on all of the last few days' events—the "waking" episodes, Otis's comments, and the conversation I'd had with Verda Mae.

"Trinity, it's time for us to make a plan of action. We have pieces of the puzzle, but we need to put them together. So what do we know so far?" he asked.

"We know that Jones owned a pair of laser cuffs and we believe the one we found in the canyon belongs to him. We know that he left town for some reason and planned to return. We don't know if the boot tip belongs to him or someone else who may have been with Jones in the canyon," I replied.

"We *think* the substance in the barrels is causing people to get sick and become comatose, but we're not one hundred percent sure if that's the case; however, we do know the barrels have been stolen and stashed somewhere. Why? Could Jones have a partnership with some unsavory characters who offered to pay for the truck and the barrels?"

"Otis thinks that we need to check out the Lost Canyon Mine. Do you know where it is? Is it big enough to hide the truck and its contents?"

"I've heard stories about the mine, but I don't know enough about it to give an opinion," he said.

"Otis said he overheard a phone call between Silas and someone who wanted to know how to locate the mine," I said.

"It sounds like we need to have a talk with Silas about that call," he said as he stood to leave.

I got up to walk him out. We were standing on the front porch listening to "Time Won't Let Me" by the Outsiders playing on the jukebox when we heard a huge explosion. It was so loud that the picture windows shook.

"Oh my goodness! What was that?" I asked.

"It sounded like it came from the edge of the city limits where the Reverence Trailer Park is."

"Let's drive down there and find out what happened," I said.

We drove to the edge of town in his truck. The closer we got, the brighter it was. We realized that an enormous blaze was burning what looked like one of the trailers in the park.

Sheriff Barnes was at the entrance to the park, waving his arms for us to stop. "Sorry, Pete, I can't let you get any closer. Verda Mae's trailer has blown up for some unknown reason. The volunteer firemen are on the way, but I don't think there's any hope of saving her home. I just pray that she and her mom were not in there when it happened," he said.

I couldn't believe what I was hearing. How could Verda Mae's house explode? Did someone cause the explosion to keep her quiet? The mystery was getting more and more complicated.

Chapter 9: The Dancing Elk Casino and the Lost Canyon Mine

Vonda's Salsa Olé

6 cans whole peeled tomatoes
1–2 onions
10 jalapeños
⅓ cup oil
⅓ cup vinegar
⅛ cup Accent (no MSG)
⅛ cup salt
1 teaspoon garlic powder
¼ teaspoon gold edge lemon thyme

Blend the tomatoes, onions, and jalapeños in a food processor.

Heat oil, vinegar, Accent, salt, and garlic powder. Let cool. Fold thyme in to tomato mix. Stir and put in jars. Refrigerate.

The entire town was buzzing about the explosion. Pete and I stopped in to ask the sheriff what or who caused the trailer to blow up.

"We know that arson was involved, but we don't have any clues as to who is responsible for the crime. The good news is that neither Verda Mae nor her mom were in the house at the time. They are safe and sound at a relative's house in Willcox. I have asked Verda Mae to come in to see if she might have any idea who would do such a thing," Sheriff Barnes said.

"When she arrives, would it be all right if I listen in on the conversation? I have a feeling that her trailer exploding might have some sort of connection to the army investigation," Pete said.

"Sure. I'll contact you as soon as I hear back from her and let you know when she's coming in," Sheriff Barnes replied. We were walking out the door to go back to the restaurant when my phone buzzed. I glanced down and saw Verda Mae's face on the screen.

"Hello, Verda Mae. I'm so sorry to hear about your home. We just left Sheriff Barnes and he said you'd be coming back to Reverence to talk about who might want to destroy your house," I said.

"I'm not coming back anytime soon. I called you to let you know that I still haven't heard from Jones, but I did get a message from Milo, one of his previous prison cellmates, asking me to meet him at the Dancing Elk Casino near Phoenix tomorrow. Jones and Milo were in the state pen together two years ago serving time for robbery. He said he had valuable information to share with me concerning Jones and his possible whereabouts. I am nervous to meet with him alone. Do you think you could break away and go with me since you're so interested in finding Jones?" she asked.

"I will have to see if I can get someone to take over my responsibilities here before I commit to a trip to Phoenix. I will call you back in a couple of hours and let you know. What time are you meeting Milo?"

"I'm meeting him at ten at night after he gets off work. He works as a dishwasher at the Dancing Elk Casino Restaurant."

"Wow, that's late, but I guess we can find a hotel to stay in for the night and head back Saturday morning."

"Thanks for thinking about traveling with me. I'll have my phone with me and look forward to you calling me back," she responded.

"Pete," I said, "Verda Mae heard from an old prison cellmate of Jones. He said he had valuable information for her. She wants me to go with her to hear what he has to say."

"When are you going?" Pete asked.

"Tomorrow, if I can get Brother Dan to cover for me at the resort and check to see if Jo Ellen and Gabe have everything under control at Southern Thyme," I replied.

"I wish I could go with you, but Colonel Heath is arriving tomorrow afternoon to find out where we are with the investigation. Please convince Verda Mae to come back here first before going to Phoenix so that she can talk to Sheriff Barnes. I know she's scared, but she needs all of us in her corner as we try to unravel this mystery," he said.

"Okay, I'll let her know that it's in her best interest," I said.

* * *

Convincing Verda Mae into coming back here was more difficult than I'd imagined. The only reason she'd agreed to talk with the sheriff was because I'd told her either she did or I wouldn't go with her to Phoenix. I promised to sit with her while she met with him. Tomorrow was going to be a long day, but hopefully a productive one.

* * *

"Verda Mae, do you know who would want to blow up your house?" Sheriff Barnes asked.

"No, I don't. I can't imagine anyone being so cruel. What would cause someone to rig my trailer to explode?" she asked, big-eyed.

"Could it be someone who has it out for Jones? Do you know what he has himself mixed up in?" he asked.

"All I know is, Jones left town and said he'd be back to celebrate a job he'd been hired to do. He acted like he'd be a millionaire or something," she replied.

"Where did he go?" Sheriff Barnes asked.

"I don't know. I'm hoping to find out more about where he might be when Trinity and I meet with his friend near Phoenix," she said curtly.

"Well, I'll expect to see you again on Monday after you return from your trip. You're mighty lucky to have Miss Trinity going with you," he said.

"I know. I appreciate her. We'll both come back and talk to you on Monday," she said as she stood up to leave.

* * *

We left town before lunch. I packed a sack lunch for us so that we could get to Phoenix by early afternoon. We'd have to find a hotel before going to the Dancing Elk Casino.

"Verda Mae, have you ever been to the casino before?" I asked.

"Yes, one time. Jones and I met Milo and a girl he was dating at the time and partied until dawn. That was before he lost his job at the Rancho del Sol," she said.

"Did he tell you why he lost his job at the ranch?"

"I asked, but he wouldn't tell me much. All he said was that he and Mr. Butler didn't see eye to eye on how to take care of the ranch. He didn't tell me he was fired, but I figured it out. Jones had a knack for getting into trouble with his bosses. He worked for Silas Warner at the resort for a short period of time before going to the ranch. I never found out what happened to cause him to leave the resort. He had a falling-out with Mr. Warner, but he called Jones not long ago and asked if he was interested in working for him again. Then all this other stuff happened," she sighed.

When we got to the hotel I called Pete.

"Pete, you're right. We've got to have a conversation with Silas as soon as I get back. I think he might give us some clues about Jones. Verda Mae said that Silas called him and asked if he wanted to work for him again. She doesn't know what he was going to be doing, but I'm curious as to why Silas wanted to work with Jones after firing him and knowing what he did when he was working for you," I said.

"I don't believe Silas offered to hire him again. Jones probably made it up to impress Verda Mae. I believe he had other plans and didn't want her to know what they were," Pete said.

"You're probably right. I'll call you again after we meet with Milo. Maybe his news will put us on Jones's trail," I said.

* * *

We decided to have dinner in the casino. The buffet was inexpensive and Milo asked us to meet him in the restaurant at ten sharp, so we took our time perusing the food items, especially the desserts. I asked our server if the chef had a few minutes to talk with us about the food choices and she said she'd ask.

"Hello, my name is Chef Henri. What questions do you have?" he asked.

"My name is Trinity and this is my friend, Verda Mae. We're looking forward to dining here this evening. I'm a restaurant owner in Reverence and I wanted to ask you about some of your buffet entrees," I answered.

"Sure. What do you want to know?" he asked.

"There are so many choices. You must have several assistants working under you to prepare all of this wonderful-looking food," I began.

"I wish I had more. One of our dishwashers is trying to move up by taking on more responsibility to prepare the salad bar," he said.

"Oh, who might your progressive dishwasher be? We're actually here to meet with one of your dishwashers after he gets off work. He's a friend of her boyfriend," I said, pointing to Verda Mae.

"Who are you meeting?" he inquired.

"His name is Milo," I said, but didn't say more because I wanted to hear what Chef Henri said and watch his body language when he heard Milo's name.

"That's him. I haven't interviewed him yet for the position. Since you're a restaurant owner, maybe you would let me know what you think about his professionalism and even ask him some questions, like how he plans to improve the salad bar at the Dancing Elk," he said.

"I'll be sure to ask him some questions and I'll get back to you tomorrow before we leave town. Is that okay?" I asked.

"I'll go get him now. My nephew is visiting and I can ask him to wash some of the dishes while you talk with Milo. That way you won't have to be out late tonight," he said as he got up to walk back into the kitchen.

"Wow, that's impressive. We just got here and you're already making friends with Milo's boss," Verda Mae said.

"I thought it might be important to have Milo know we are interested in his well-being. That way he'll be more apt to tell us truthful information rather than send us on some wild goose chase," I said.

Milo walked toward us and put out his hand for us to shake. "Hi, ladies. My boss said I could meet with you early so here I am," he said.

"I know you asked to talk to Verda Mae, but she wanted me to tag along to hear what you have to share with her. My name is Trinity. I own a restaurant in Reverence and have an interest in where Jones Chancellor might be. I'll just cut to the chase. Is he involved in the missing army truck, driver, and barrels, and if so, does he know why so many people are getting sick?" I asked.

"All I know is he wanted me to help him relocate that truck and transfer the barrels to another location. He told me I'd make a lot of money if I helped him. I was on my way to the canyon when I heard about Walt's and Lois's illnesses. I decided I didn't want anything to do with those barrels and the contents in them. So I didn't go. I called Jones back, but my call went to his voicemail. I haven't heard from him since," Milo said.

"And you were supposed to meet him at Whispering Breeze Canyon?" I asked.

"Yes, he knew about some old mine that he could hide the truck in until we found a way to transfer the barrels, but I don't know exactly where the mine is. He was going to meet me at the entrance of the canyon after dark," he said.

I pulled two objects out of my purse. "Milo, take a look at these. Do they belong to Jones?"

"The laser cuff looks like his, but the boot tip doesn't look familiar."

"Thanks for the information. Now tell me how you plan to make the Dancing Elk salad bar the best in the state of Arizona?" I asked.

* * *

I called Pete and told him what we'd found out.

"Trinity, we've got to find out where that mine is! When you get home, let's talk with Silas immediately about the location," he said.

By the time I arrived back in Reverence, Otis was on the front porch of the restaurant, pacing.

"You're home! I've rented a hover car for us to drive to the canyon. Did you know they can fly up into the air and hover just like a helicopter?" he asked.

"No, I don't know much about them. Where on earth did you find one?" I asked.

"One of the resort's customers is investing in a company that owns them. He flew to the Reverence airport in it. I asked him if he'd let us rent it for the day. He's leaving first thing in the morning, so we have to go now if we want to find the mine," he said.

"I think I need to wait for Pete to get out of his meeting with the colonel and let him go with us," I said.

"I found a map that Silas had in his desk top drawer and it shows exactly where the mine is. We can go see if it's where the map shows and report back to Pete. He can return with us later," Otis said.

Even though I knew we should wait for Pete, I agreed to go with Otis. "Okay, we'll go see if we can find the entrance, but then we'll turn around and come back to give a report to Pete," I said.

We started driving the hover car and then Otis pushed a button and we were suddenly in the air.

"How did you know which button to push?" I asked.

"People think I don't know much, but when it comes to mechanical things, I know plenty. The owner gave me a lesson on the controls," he said.

I looked at the map Otis had and directed him to the spot where the entrance of the mine was supposed to be. We couldn't see any doorway or cave entrance. We decided to land and get out and walk to see what was visible on the ground.

We walked a few feet and then we were falling through a hole in the ground.

* * *

When I woke up, I only saw light coming from above us. Otis was lying beside me and seemed to be knocked out.

"Otis, are you all right?" I asked.

He moaned and turned over. "Trinity, take the flashlights out of my bag that's beside me. We have to see where we are. This has to be one of the mine corridors. The map must have led us to the top of the mine, not the entrance. We must have fallen through soft ground and are now in a shaft of the mine."

I got the flashlights and we looked up above, where we could see how far the opening was. It looked like we'd dropped around fifteen feet. The ground around us was wet and I could see puddles along the tunnel to our right. We got up and started walking down the corridor. It was a good thing Otis had thought to bring the flashlights. Without them we wouldn't be able to see anything.

"Otis, look, is that the front of a big truck up ahead? Do you think it's the missing army truck?" I asked.

Before he could answer, the walls of the tunnel started shaking and there was dust all around us.

Otis pushed me down and covered me with his body. The last thing I saw was the earth caving in on us. How would we get out of this alive?

Chapter 10: The Lost Mine Rescue

Elizabeth's Salsa Thyme
1 28-oz. can whole peeled tomatoes
1 cayenne pepper, seeded
1 7-oz. can green chilies
1 bunch fresh cilantro, stems cut off
½ teaspoon garlic salt
¼ teaspoon caraway thyme
½ diced onion (optional)
Blend all together. Refrigerate. Enjoy!

The following is an account of Pete's memories of the Lost Mine rescue:

"Silas, do you have time to talk with me for a few minutes? I'm sorry to show up here unannounced, but Trinity is missing and I need to see if you or Otis knows where she might be."

"Come in, Pete. You just caught me. I was on my way into town to see if Otis is with Trinity."

"Otis is gone, too?"

"I checked the stables to see if he was with his donkeys, but he's not. Let's go over to the resort and talk to Brother Dan. He might know where they both are," Silas said emphatically.

* * *

When we got to the resort, Silas approached Brother Dan. "Good afternoon, Dan. Have you seen Trinity or Otis lately?"

"They're not back? Trinity asked me to take charge here for a couple of hours while she went on a ride with Otis, but that was over four hours ago. I heard Otis say something about a hover car. Do you know what that is?" Dan asked.

"One of our residents flew one to the airport yesterday. I'll connect with him on the room monitor to see what he knows… Sid, this is Silas. Did Otis take your hover car somewhere?"

"Yes, he asked to borrow it for a couple of hours. He wanted to show someone a place he'd discovered on a map—Lost Canyon?"

"Lost Mine?" Silas asked.

"Yes, that's it. They should be back by now. Check with the Hangar Ten supervisor and find out if they brought it back or not."

"Thanks, Sid. We will."

* * *

The hover car was not back, but the hangar supervisor was able to tell us its location on his screen. Silas and I traveled to the spot he told us about in Whispering Breeze Canyon. Before leaving the airport, I called Colonel Heath and told him about the Lost Mine, and asked him to meet us with army personnel and rescue equipment.

How had Silas known they'd gone to find the Lost Mine? I had a sick feeling that something must have happened to Trinity and Otis, since they hadn't called and let us know where they were.

* * *

We arrived about an hour before sunset. The hover car was there, but no one was in it. Silas and I got out of the truck and walked around it, hoping to glean some clue as to where they'd gone. As soon as we got in front of the car, we both saw the gigantic hole about ten feet wide up ahead.

"Oh, no! Please tell me you don't think they fell down that hole in the ground," Silas gasped.

As we got closer, I could tell that this wasn't a good situation. Peering down, I saw the mine floor, but again couldn't see Trinity or Otis lying at the bottom.

“Do you think they fell through this hole?” Silas asked.

“If they did, where are they now?” I cupped my hands around my mouth and hollered, “Trinity, Otis, where are you?”

I paused for a few seconds and then yelled again, but there wasn’t any response.Colonel Heath and his army crew arrived and joined us at the opening. I looked up and saw a black helicopter in the sky. He’d brought a Black Hawk helicopter with him. I had heard about the army’s Black Hawk. It was a four-bladed, twin-engine tactical transport machine. I was thankful the colonel had thought to bring it with the rest of his crew.

“We’ll unload the equipment and let some men cable down to search where the mine leads. Surely they’re down there somewhere. We must be careful not to cause a cave-in when we descend. Let me talk to my second in command about the research he did on the mine before we go down.”

Colonel Heath walked to the first army vehicle in line and conferred with another officer. I was listening in on their conversation when I noticed Silas wasn’t standing beside me.

One of the other officers came running up, shouting, “Colonel, that other civilian must have grabbed a cable out of the supply truck, because one is missing.”

We all ran to the hole and shined our high-powered flashlights down to see Silas standing at the bottom.

"What are you doing, Silas?" I yelled.

"It's my fault they're down here and it's my responsibility to find them. Please don't follow me. The more people are down here, the more likely it is that the walls will come crashing down."

"He's right, Pete. All we can do now is wait for him to return, hopefully with your friends in tow," Colonel Heath remarked.

It seemed like an eternity before we heard or saw anyone. Finally, after about an hour, we heard Silas call, "I found them! They're both shaken up and have a few cuts and bruises, but they're alive and I'm sending them up." He'd had the forethought to tie the cable to the hitch on one of the supply trucks.

I couldn't believe it! Trinity came up first and then Otis. We were all crying and hugging each other.

Just when Trinity started to speak we heard a loud explosion and were pelted with dirt and gravel. We watched the debris skyrocket up out of the hole.

Colonel Heath screamed, "Take cover!"

We fell to the ground and put our hands over our heads as the rocks and other debris continued to rain down on us. Just as soon as it had begun, it was over. We stood up and looked back toward the opening in the ground. It was almost gone. How could that have happened?

* * *

Trinity's memory of the rescue:

Otis and I were sitting behind the rocks that had fallen in on the mine floor, trying to figure out what our next move would be, when we heard Silas calling our names.

"Trinity! Otis! Are you down here?"

"Yes, we're on the other side of what must be in front of you," I replied.

"Great to hear your voice, Trinity. I brought down a pickaxe and some other stuff in a backpack. Hold on. I'll get you out of there."

"Silas, I'm sorry for not telling you about taking the hover car," Otis said.

"We'll talk about that later, Otis. I'm just glad you're alive. Now stand back while I work on getting you out."

Thirty minutes later we were walking back the way we'd come in. It was a blessing to look up and see Pete's face. He and his army friend pulled us up one at a time. We were caught up in the rescue celebration and didn't notice that Silas hadn't come up.

Without warning the ground started to tremble as an earthquake destroyed the place we'd just left. Minutes later we were standing and staring at a narrow hole. Silas had rescued us, but was he going to be alive and in one piece when we found him?

The Black Hawk helicopter pilot took us to be checked over at the resort. I'd never heard of the transport unit. The copilot told us the helicopter was named after a Native American war leader from the Sauk Indian tribe. We were so fortunate to have them be a part of the rescue team.

* * *

Silas didn't make it. The army was able to find the cave entrance to the mine after I told them what I'd seen before the first cave-in. Inside they discovered the truck and barrels, one of which was turned over, seeping a toxic substance onto the bed of the trailer.

The good news was that the men who went in had on hazmat suits that kept them safe. The bad news was that they not only found the overturned barrel, but also discovered three bodies—Jones Chancellor, the driver, and, a few feet down the corridor, Silas, covered in a mound of rocks and gravel. He must have gone in the opposite direction from the rescue site. Obviously he'd seen the truck and decided to investigate why it was there. We would always remember how Silas saved our lives at the expense of his own.

* * *

Riding back to the resort in silence, we were in shock. Otis was especially quiet. My heart ached for him. Silas had been with him literally since birth and now he was gone.

I walked him into his house and sat with him for a while. Again, the silence was deafening. Just when I was going to see if he wanted me to make him something to eat, he said, "Trinity, Silas wouldn't leave without some final word of comfort. Walk with me to his office to see if he wrote a note or left something to let me know it is going to be okay."

We walked to the office and peered at the contents on the desk. Sure enough, there was an envelope with Otis's name on it.

"You open it and read what's inside to me. I can't do it."

I did as he instructed. I read a few lines silently, then hesitated. Would Otis be all right once I read what Silas had to say? His last words would forever haunt us!

Dear Otis (& Trinity),

If you're reading this, I'm either dead or severely injured. Whatever the circumstance, it's important I explain things to you that are bothering me.

First of all, I owe you and everyone I know an apology. I've known what has been happening to our sleeping friends and others for a long time.

How? A couple of months ago, I was approached by one of our previous residents. He was a contractor for a foreign government and wanted me to help him purchase and transport a toxic waste formula created by our US Army.

We needed the money so I agreed to intercept the formula. Back when I made the decision to open the resort, I took out a loan to make it the best it could be. Unfortunately, I invested the borrowed money into a no-fail-get-rich scheme, but it totally failed. So I borrowed more money from some shady people who charged a high interest to make the resort grand opening happen. Needless to say, I got further and further into debt.

Thinking about leaving you with this burden was painful for me, especially since I recently found out I have a brain tumor and at most have six months to live.

I never wanted anyone to get hurt, much less as sick as some people have. The guilt is unbearable. Please know I had nothing to do with Verda Mae's trailer exploding. I think the man who paid me to get the truck thought he'd been double-crossed by Jones and was trying to send him a message.

My hope is that a cure is developed, and everyone will regain consciousness and live to be old surrounded by grandkids and great-grandkids.

Trinity, you've been a blessing in our lives and such an asset to Reverence. Please check in on Otis when you can, and thank you for your love for our community.

Otis, stand tall and continue to be the reason people visit the Oasis Resort. I love you!

Your brother (& friend),

Silas

Once I finished reading, I folded the letter, put it back into the envelope, and placed it on the desk.

"Otis, I'm so sorry for your loss. I'm here for you today and always."

He put his arms out and I went to him and gave him the biggest hug ever.

Chapter 11: The Awakening Celebration & A Wedding

Tres Amigas Avocado-Cilantro Sauce
1 ripe avocado
1 small handful cilantro
1 sprig ruby thyme, crushed
¼ cup grapeseed oil
½ garlic clove
Sea salt to taste
Water to blend

Pour everything in a blender and puree on high until smooth and creamy.

Add as much water as you need to get a pourable consistency or less for dipping sauce. Pair with chips or any favorite food.

Silas's life-insurance money provided for Otis's future. He inherited the resort and the land around it. He planned to hire cowboys and cowgirls to perform tricks for families staying at the resort. He wanted to call it *Rodeo Days at the Oasis.* Slim Pickens would be his partner and would follow in the footsteps of his namesake by being a rodeo performer himself.

The army tied up all the loose ends. Silas had hired Jones to intercept the truck and park it in the Lost Mine storage facility until they could find a way to move the barrels to another hidden building. Their last meeting was in the Whispering Breeze Canyon. Jones had dropped one of his cufflinks when walking around the area and Silas must have tripped over a rock, causing his boot tip to come off. Otis identified it as one belonging to Silas.

Colonel Heath speculated that the barrel had overturned when the driver was trying to back up into the facility, but upon closer inspection it turned out that the lid had never been tightened appropriately on the overturned barrel; therefore, the lid popped open and the toxic liquid spilled out onto the truck trailer floor. Jones must have closed the hidden door prior to falling asleep. He and the driver died within twelve hours, according to the medical examiner. The driver died first since the fumes were already affecting him while the truck was moving down the highway to the mine.

Toxic fumes apparently blew into Reverence and surrounding areas before he ever got to the canyon. That was why he'd called and said he was lightheaded.

The invisible fumes continued to blow with the wind before the door was sealed, triggering the catastrophic effects that made some people catatonic and eventually put them in a deep sleep.

The army was able to get the contents back to their lab; therefore, the scientists cultivated a cure for all those infected. Thyme was added to enhance the awakening experience. Everyone was up and about now—smiling, asking questions, and wanting to share their good fortune with family and friends.

Verda Mae moved into Willcox with her mom. She said she needed a new start, especially since she didn't have a house anymore in Reverence. She promised to visit every now and then.

I picked up where I'd left off at the restaurant. Otis and Pete came in every morning for breakfast and conversation. When they left each day, Otis would wave and smile, saying, "See you in the morning."

Pete would always pause before going out the door, turn and smile, then tip his hat in my direction. I had a feeling he and I were going to spend more and more time together in the future.

* * *

The staff and I decided to put together an Awakening Celebration at Southern Thyme Catering Company.

Lois helped plan the festivities. We honored the affected people by selling tickets to table sponsors.

The first table was reserved for Walt, his sister, Becca, Saydi, Maia, and Zoë. Lois was surrounded by her bridge buddies—Billye, Suzanne, and Jimmie. Others from Reverence were lovingly joined by Brother Dan, Jo Ellen, Gabe, Mary Tom, Pete, Otis, and me.

Brother Dan told us how his mom named him after the prophet Daniel, and then read two verses from the book of Daniel, 6:26–27: "For he is the living God and he endures forever; his kingdom will not be destroyed, his dominion will never end, he rescues and he saves; he performs signs and wonders in the heavens and on the earth."

Lois closed the evening with a flag dance to "Love Lifted Me":

Love lifted me, love lifted me. When nothing else would do, love lifted me…

Love lifted me, love lifted me. When I was down and out, love lifted me.

After that, we broke out into one of my favorites, "Time Is on my Side" by the Rolling Stones.

"Thyme" was on our side, just as Otis had predicted. We continued to sing, clap, and hug each other until the wee hours of the morning. Then we all went out to the front porch and watched the sunrise. What a glorious day it turned out to be!

* * *

It was hard to believe that our Awakening Celebration was six months ago. We were all gathered again for another special event—my wedding!

Pete had asked me to marry him a few days after the celebration. He invited me to the ranch for supper, the meal he calls "dinner." We were sitting on the back porch grilling steaks and watching the sun set behind the Cochise County mountain range when he said, "Trinity, I have something to ask you."

"Okay, ask."

"Will you give me the honor of spending time on this porch every evening?"

"Pete, what are you trying to tell me? Do you want me to move to the ranch and live in your bunkhouse?"

"No, I'd rather you live in the ranch house with me as my wife." He turned his head and smiled at me with tears in his eyes.

"Well, alrighty then. I will."

* * *

Brother Dan performed the wedding ceremony of my dreams. He quoted 1 Corinthians 13:13: "And now these three remain: faith, hope and love. But the greatest of these is love."

Becca was my maid of honor and Otis was Pete's best man. We were surrounded by all our family and friends. It was a perfect day for us and one we'd never forget.

Pete thought it would be fun to have a wedding march from the church to the restaurant where we had our reception. Otis asked me if I would like to ride Frosty down the street with Pete walking beside me. He was so excited about the possibility, I couldn't say no.

Frosty and I led the procession with everyone else following us. The praise band from church came along to play music as we marched. Everything was going as planned until we got to the restaurant. The front door was open and when Pete lifted me off Frosty and I walked up to the door, I saw Otis's four mini burros inside. The first thing I noticed was that the wedding cake was intact; however, looking around the room, I discovered the vegetable trays were turned over on the floor with no vegetables on them. Obviously Cici, Pal, Fig, and sweet little Valentine had had a feast before we arrived.

"I'm so sorry, Trinity! I thought I locked the trailer before I went to the church," Otis said.

Instead of getting upset, I replied, “Who would want to eat healthy snacks anyway on their wedding day? It’s all about the cake and the cake is just fine.”

Grandma Cora came up and stood beside me, again laughing so hard she was crying. “We wouldn’t want to have your wedding reception any other way. The Trinity women always have the most exciting adventures before and after they get hitched!”

“Yes, they do!” I laughed hysterically too, tears flowing down my face.

Epilogue

December 2042

Dear Mom and Grandma Cora,

It was such a blessing to have all of you here for the wedding. It's difficult to believe that we've already been married three months! I have some exciting news. A new bookstore has opened downtown in Reverence. It's called A New Chapter—Books on the Square, owned by a mother and daughter, Shirley and Sarah. The store is conveniently located next to the museum in an old warehouse. They meet at the restaurant each week with their book-club friends. I love the literary culture that is being established in this community!

Pete and I are enjoying our lives here, especially at Rancho del Sol. Between our chores on the ranch and taking care of the day-to-day business at the restaurant, we really don't have time for anything else. Of course, you two have always made your children and grandchildren a priority even when you had lots of "irons in the fire." Therefore, I am following in your footsteps. My children will definitely be number one in my life. In case you haven't already guessed by now, I have some more exciting news: Pete and I are expecting twins in July! We found out that they are girls and we're more than thrilled about them joining the Trinity women line.

Their names will be Betsy Grace and Tallulah Belle. I have such fond memories of the stories you shared about Betsy and her best friend, Tallulah. We hope that one or both will be renowned pastry chefs, even though I believe only Tallulah was gifted in that area in the past. If there's something that all the Trinity women have in common, it's faith, family, and the love of food. I will close with one of my favorite verses that you had me memorize at a very early age and one that I will teach my girls one day:

"May the words of my mouth and the meditation of my heart be pleasing in your sight, Lord, my Rock and my Redeemer" (Psalm 19:14).

Thanks for showing me what it means to love the Lord and others!

Love that never fails!

Trinity

A New
Chapter
Books
on the
Square

Made in the USA
Lexington, KY
09 November 2018